MONSTERS ON THE BEACH

Anthony Masters

Teddy looked towards the dark shape of Sea Spit Nuclear Power Station, looming immediately above them. "You mark my words, they're making monsters."

Tim is the newest member of Green Watch – an environmental pressure group founded by his uncle, Seb Howard, and his two kids, Brian and Flower. Together they battle to protect the natural world from ruthless exploitation – campaigning against the needless slaughter of innocent creatures and the thoughtless pollution of the environment. No animal is too small for Green Watch to care about and no place too remote for them to get to. Needless to say, they manage to ruffle quite a few feathers along the way . . .

MONSTERS ON THE BEACH

by
Anthony Masters
Illustrated by Pauline Hazelwood

Hippo Books
Scholastic Publications Limited
London

Scholastic Publications Ltd.,
10 Earlham Street, London WC2H 9RX, UK

Scholastic Inc.,
730 Broadway, New York, NY 10003, USA

Scholastic Tab Publications Ltd.,
123 Newkirk Road, Richmond Hill,
Ontario L4C 3G5, Canada

Ashton Scholastic Pty Ltd.,
P O Box 579, Gosford, New South Wales,
Australia

Ashton Scholastic Ltd.,
165 Marua Road, Panmure, Auckland 6,
New Zealand

First published in the UK by Scholastic Publications Ltd., 1990

ISBN 0 590 76353 9

Typeset by AKM Associates (UK) Ltd., Southall, London
Printed by Cox and Wyman Ltd., Reading, Berks
10 9 8 7 6 5 4 3 2 1

To Mark, Vicky, Simon and Robina
– with much love –

Chapter One

The wind had reached screaming point and the waves crashing on the pebbles made a grinding roar as the undertow pulled them back. The beach shelved steeply, and around it the Northumbrian cliffs looked black as slate. The Nuclear Power Station stood out bleakly in the moonlight, its reactor and cooling towers pallidly distinct.

Crouched in the old drying shed and hardly daring to breathe, Seb, Tim, Flower and Brian waited for the Reapers. They had already been there for over an hour and Tim, like the others, was suffering from awful cramp. It was agony and all the time getting worse. What was more he longed to sneeze, cough, clear his throat or scratch and he was sure that at some point he was going to scream out in rage and frustration.

He looked round at the others; they were as still and as silent as statues, but he was sure they were hurting inside. Or were they? He remembered how they had once watched badgers.* It seemed hundreds of years ago now instead of just about a year. What had Mr Andrews told them to do? Swallow themselves? It seemed ridiculous but Tim knew how much it had helped. He tried to imagine doing it again – swallowing himself so he lay inside the shell of his body. But the cramp stayed. Perhaps it was because he had so much wanted to see the badgers that he had really tried to adopt Mr Andrews' advice. But the last thing he wanted to do was to see the Reapers.

Flower nudged him. Someone – some people – were coming. Immediately he experienced a spark of fear that killed everything else he was feeling. They were here.

Six men, dressed in sou'westers and huddled against the wind, battered their way along the beach. They stared down at the pebbles as they went, examining flotsam, sea cabbage and kale, flashing a guarded torch occasionally into a rock pool, searching, searching. Tim shivered. They were an incredible sight, these night-time scavengers. But it was what they were looking for that was so appalling, as well as what they would do to the four members of Green Watch if they were discovered. The Reapers walked on past them, boots scrunching on the pebbles,

* *Battle for the Badgers* – Book One in the Green Watch Series

heading towards Sea Spit, the power station – the ominous place that Teddy was so sure was creating the monsters on the beach. But they would come back, Tim was certain, for they had arrived in a small truck that was parked over by the lifeboat station, just behind the trawlers that were drawn up on their winches, high on the beach.

Tim glanced at his watch. It was just after 2 am on this wild and windy October night. The cramp started to return as the fear began to recede and the wait became eternal again – this time for them to come back. Then, with enormous relief, he heard their shuffling steps against the howling wind – and they were gone. Minutes later, he dimly heard the van start up again, but its progress was lost in the wind. He turned to Seb but his uncle put his finger to his lips, motioning Tim to keep silent and still. They must have stayed frozen for another agonising ten minutes until Seb decided it was safe to move outside. Cautiously, he went first and then beckoned them to follow.

It was wonderful to stand up, to move around, to feel the wind on his face. Tim stretched in elation.

"We didn't see much," said Seb gloomily. "There wasn't much to see."

"What would they do if they found a bunch of monster crabs, Dad?" asked Brian.

"Kill them, I s'pose – and hide the remains."

"I bet they don't even exist," said Flower irritably.

Tim was inclined to agree but decided to keep quiet.

"Then why the Reapers?" asked Seb unanswerably.

No one felt like going to bed when they got back to the old railway carriage further up the beach that was Teddy Cormack's home. It was set in a break in the cliffs and next to it was the boarded-up snack bar that the council had licensed Teddy to run in the summer season. He had been living in the railway carriage for as long as any of the locals could remember, and had had dozens of different occupations ranging from fisherman to cook in a nearby hotel and from boatbuilder to tally man. Why the council had ever agreed to him living in the railway carriage was never clear. Perhaps they hadn't; he had been there so long it was impossible to say.

"Well?"

"Nothing," replied Seb.

"You mean they didn't come?"

"Oh yes, they came all right. They sleuthed up and down the beach and took off in their van."

Teddy looked disappointed. He was old and weatherbeaten, with a round rosy-cheeked face and an unkempt, straggly grey beard that was often stained with soup or gravy or even, as Tim had noticed once, jam.

"Did you get a look at the beach yourselves?" Teddy persisted.

"Well, before they came."

"Anything unusual?"

"No."

The old man was obviously crushingly disappointed. Then he looked more cheerful.

"Anne will be back tomorrow morning," he muttered. "She'll have a careful look."

"Meaning we didn't?" asked Flower indignantly. Her father Seb had only just got married again – to Anne, who was in London helping to set up a Dolphin Protection Society for the Devon and Cornish coast. Just after their adventure in Cornwall* Anne, a professional diver and naturalist, had married Seb. At first Flower had resented their relationship, because to her at least, no one could replace her mother who had divorced her father some years ago. But now she saw Anne as a friend, not as a mother, and Brian felt the same. Until Tim had joined and proved himself, Green Watch had been a trio. Now it was a quintet.

Teddy Cormack thought highly of Anne, mainly because he had not bent her ear as much as he had Seb's and she was still prepared to listen to him. So he didn't answer Flower, which made her even more angry. Teddy could be like that, thought Tim. Cantankerous. And Green Watch had embarked on their fourth adventure, risking everything on what Teddy had told them.

"Who wants cocoa?" he asked grudgingly.

They all did and he went out grumpily to make it. The kitchen was right down the other end of the

---

* *Dolphin's Revenge* – Book Three in the Green Watch Series

5

carriage and once Teddy was safely out of earshot, Seb spoke quietly and authoritatively.

"We could be wasting our time," he said flatly.

"You're tired, Dad.' Brian didn't sound very confident.

"On the contrary – I'm wide awake."

"You mean you think Teddy made it all up?" asked Tim incredulously.

"He could have imagined it."

"Giant claws and sea cabbages?" enquired Flower impatiently.

"He'll be back in a minute. Let's run over it again. Sea Spit has had two scares in a year – leaks that their people say have caused no excess radiation at all. They've been the subject of an enquiry, and been cleared."

"Whitewashed more likely," said Brian. Of all the members of Green Watch he had always been the one most concerned by the dangers the nuclear power station represented. There were so many instances of cancer and leukaemia in the vicinity that it must be more than a coincidence – he had always been sure of it. He had also convinced Tim. But Seb and Flower hadn't entirely made up their minds. Yet.

"Well, we don't know," continued Seb. "All we do know is that Teddy is having a running battle with Sea Spit, and Anne got to hear about it. That's why we're here – to see if there's anything in Teddy's accusations. And in my opinion there's nothing."

Teddy's accusations had been quite something, thought Tim uneasily. He claimed that the sea plants on the beach and foreshore were growing to an enormous size, that he had seen giant crabs emerging from the water. He was accusing Philip Watson, head of Public Relations at Sea Spit, of employing a squad of fishermen to comb the beach at night and ensure everything out of the ordinary was removed. Teddy had grimly nicknamed them the Reapers.

"But they *are* combing the beach," said Brian testily. "Surely that proves something?"

"It *is* odd. They're obviously looking for something, and it's all very furtive. But I don't think they're looking for giant plants or crabs."

"Then what are they looking for?" demanded Flower.

"I just don't know," replied Seb.

"That's what we're here to find out," said Brian. "Surely."

"It's not much to base an investigation on, and we've been here two days already. This is half-term, Brian, not a month's holiday."

"So you mean all Green Watch investigations have to be squeezed into the holidays?" snapped Brian.

Seb groaned. "Don't start losing your cool, Brian."

"I'm not."

"You know damn well I've got at least half a dozen investigations on right now. There's the business with the wild cats in the East End, the Marsh in Essex, that phoney bird sanctuary in—"

"Sorry, Dad."

"Eh?"

"Dad, I'm apologising. I'm sorry. I know I don't do it very often but I'm apologising now." He grinned.

So did Seb. Tim was relieved. He hated any friction in Green Watch. It was a difficult time for Tim. His father, Seb's brother, was shortly to be released from prison and Tim was wondering how difficult it was going to be, getting to know him properly again. While he was with Green Watch, Tim felt secure despite the dangerous projects they got involved in. But now he would have to face up to having a real family of his own all over again.

"You're right, Brian. The Reapers are a mysterious bunch. What the hell can they be looking for? But that's *all* we've got as evidence – a bunch of men searching a beach."

"Every night?" commented Flower drily.

"So Teddy says."

"Well, we've seen them tonight," put in Tim.

"Yes," Seb nodded. "But we can't spend time on this. At least I can't. The other projects are too pressing. Anne will be back tomorrow morning, and I need to help her with the Dolphin Trust." He paused and looked at Brian. Then he said, "I know what you're going to say."

"Well done, Dad."

"Go on and say it then."

"Let us take over. That'll give you and Anne time to handle the other things. We'll manage. At least we've got a deadline – like the end of half term."

Seb looked at him uneasily. "I've brought this on myself."

"Well?" Flower looked at him steadily.

"And the old boy will be livid."

"We can say we're holding the fort, building up evidence," said Tim tentatively.

"Can we?" asked Brian.

"Look." Seb made up his mind. "I've got an idea. I don't know why I didn't put it into operation earlier. I'll go and confront Watson."

"Tell him we've seen the Reapers?" asked Flower.

"Well, now we've seen them I can demand an explanation."

"Suppose he won't give one?" Brian was unimpressed.

"Then I'll alert the local police. Ask them what's going on."

"That won't do you any good," said Teddy, coming in suddenly with a slopped tray of cocoa. Tim wondered how long he had been listening out there, and what he had heard.

Seb didn't seem to care, however. "Without evidence, what else can I do, Teddy?" he snapped. "I haven't seen your giant crabs, your huge sea cabbages. Where are they now?"

"They've been taken away," he said crossly. "Taken by the Reapers."

Seb groaned again.

Next morning Green Watch woke late to find Teddy

gone and Anne in his place in the kitchen. Tim was first up so he filled her in on what had been going on. When he had finished, Anne said:

"So Seb's going to bale out?"

"Leaving us to get on with the job."

"I'm not sure that's very wise," she said, frying some bread. "The Reapers sound dodgy to me – bunch of men going up and down the beach every night."

"But that's the only mystery," yawned Tim. "We've only got Teddy's word for the rest of it."

"And that's not exactly reliable," she replied. "Not in my experience of him."

"You think he's lying?"

"No. Just getting wound up."

"Which leaves the Reapers."

"And what's Seb going to do about them?"

"He went into Sea Spit early this morning, to demand an explanation."

Anne grinned. "Doesn't that man ever get a night's sleep?"

"He's thorough, I suppose," said Tim vaguely.

"Maybe. But he's becoming a workaholic. Know how many other investigations he's got on?"

"He was telling us."

"So you'll be relieved he's leaving you to it?"

Tim looked up at her, disconcerted. "What do you mean?"

"You know what I mean, Tim."

He sighed. "I s'pose he's been getting – a bit irritable."

"He's got too much on."

"At least Green Watch has really taken off now. You should be pleased."

"I am. I'm proud to be part of it too—" She looked at him fondly. "But I still feel a raw newcomer. Did you ever feel that?"

"You bet I did! They took me climbing the first time. And I was so scared I froze to the rock face. Literally. They must have thought I was a right fool. But you'll be all right. I mean, you're a diver."

"I'm still the new girl. You're all so close."

"You're married to Seb."

"Maybe. But not to Green Watch. I'm still on probation."

"You'll soon work your way in."

"Will I?" She seemed doubtful. "I'm worried about him. He's got so much on. We've no time to ourselves at all. It's as if – something's driving him along."

Tim was pleased that she was confiding in him but he didn't really know what to say. Then he thought of something important. "He takes it all personally—" he began.

"Like he can save the world?" Anne asked, without a hint of sarcasm in her voice.

"Well, maybe that's the way he sees it."

"Then he's on an ego trip."

"No – he really believes we're all destroying the world. And that not enough's being done about it."

"If he goes on in this way," said Anne, 'he'll kill himself."

"Can't you get him to take a holiday?"

She laughed hollowly. "You try."

Seb didn't come back. By two in the afternoon, when he still hadn't returned, Anne phoned Sea Spit. Tim, Brian and Flower sat gloomily in what passed as Teddy's "lounge". It was a long narrow room that took up about half of the battered old railway carriage. It was crammed with objects from the sea-shore – shells, stones, fossils, dried seaweed, gnarled and twisted bits of wood – all the trophies of the beachcomber. A huge skeleton of a fish's head, a whale-bone, miscellaneous teeth, the name-plates of wrecked boats littered the shelves, but no one looked at anything. Even Teddy was quiet and despondent, tense now as they all listened to Anne's indistinct voice on the telephone in the kitchen. Then she put the receiver down with a sharp click and they waited anxiously as she hurried up the passage.

"He never got there."

"What?"

"He never got to Sea Spit. Seb didn't make his appointment."

"Maybe Dad got on to a new lead," said Flower hopefully.

"Driving a kilometre up the beach road?" asked Brian sceptically.

"Maybe he saw something," said Tim.

"What?" Brian asked unhelpfully.

"How do *I* know?"

They all stared helplessly at each other.

Then the doorbell rang and Teddy shuffled off to open it.

"Blimey!" he exclaimed. "It's the Old Bill."

Chapter Two

The young policeman stood self-consciously on the threshold and Tim noticed there was something very set about his face as they crowded round the narrow doorway.

"Mrs Anne Howard?"

"Yes." Her voice trembled slightly.

"I'm afraid there's been an accident."

"God, no!"

"Who?" yelled Flower.

"A Mr Sebastian Howard."

"Is he—" began Flower.

"He's hurt bad. Badly injured. In Morpeth General."

"He's not going to die, is he?" asked Brian, while Tim simply stood there, shaking all over.

"They said to come quick," replied the young policeman. "I can't tell you any more. If you want to squeeze into the car I can put the siren on. Get there quicker."

"I'll stay," said Teddy flatly. "Ring me."

"OK." Anne hurried to the car, followed by the others. In a few seconds, the siren was screaming and they were heading for Morpeth General.

"This way." The nurse marched briskly along the polished floor and stopped at a double door marked *Intensive Care Unit*. Tim felt sick. Was this the end? Was Seb toing to die? "You'll have to go in one at a time," she said in a hushed, reverent voice.

"How is he?" asked Anne falteringly.

"Very poorly," said the nurse.

"Will he live?"

"We're doing our best to make him comfortable," was the bleak reply.

"I *said*, will he live?" Anne snapped. She looked as if she was going to break down at any moment.

"You'll have to see the doctor."

"Where *is* the doctor?"

"He's in the unit." The nurse pursed her lips. Anne pushed past her, saying, "You lot wait there. I shan't be long.'

She wasn't, but the waiting seemed like an eternity as the three of them sat on a bench in the corridor. Then she was back, staring in front of her, her face flushed and tears in her eyes.

"The doctor says he'll pull through,' she said. "But it may take a while."

"Hallo, Seb!"

Seb was lying on a bed in the centre of the floor, wired up to a battery of tubes. Behind him dials were bathed in a half-light glow, a machine bleeped and what looked like a graph rose and fell on a screen. There were marks on his face and his head was swathed in bandages. A nurse sat beside him and Tim felt acutely self-conscious.

Seb opened his eyes and gave Tim a pale, lop-sided grin.

"Sorry," he said weakly, and his eyes closed again.

"You'll be fine." Tim's voice was firm. "You've got to concentrate on getting better."

The nurse motioned Tim to go and he moved reluctantly towards the door. Seb opened his eyes.

"I – I – keep seeing – Loner!"*

Tim didn't know what to say.

"Dolphin . . ." Seb mumbled.

Tim nodded. "Yes, he's a dolphin."

The nurse stood up. 'He's got to go now, Mr Howard."

"Who – are – you?" asked Seb.

"You know who I am." She whispered to Tim: "He's a bit confused."

"See you soon,' said Tim, taking Seb's hand. It

* *Dolphin's Revenge*

16

was very hot and dry.

It was after five and Anne, Tim, Flower and Brian sat drinking milky tea from a WVS stall just outside Casualty.

"Is he really going to be all right?" asked Flower for the umpteenth time.

"Yes," said Anne. She seemed much calmer now.

"So what happened?" asked Brian impatiently.

"He was carved up – on the road. Run into the ditch and the Landrover turned over."

"Who by?"

"He didn't see much of what hit him. But it was a van of some kind."

"The Reapers," said Tim.

She shrugged. "It didn't stop."

"What about the police?" asked Flower.

"As the young copper said, they're looking. But Seb's too confused to give any proper information. He can't even remember the colour of the van, let alone the number plate."

"So what are you going to do?" Flower sounded bleak. "I mean, doesn't this give the Sea Spit project a bit of priority?"

"It certainly does," said Anne.

In the end it was decided that Anne would stay overnight at the hospital and the other three should go back to Teddy's railway carriage. By the time they arrived, trailing in disconsolately, it was well after seven and the beach was in shadow. The lights in the railway carriage were on and as they tramped up to the door, Flower exclaimed:

"He's got someone with him."

They paused. Sure enough, Teddy was sitting at the rickety table in the "lounge". He was facing a man in a suit with a bald patch at the back of his head.

"Maybe it's the police," said Brian. "Plain clothes," he added doubtfully.

"Let's find out." Flower banged on the door, obviously feeling exhausted.

After a long delay Teddy opened it, looking sly. He put a finger to his lips. "Got a bloke from Sea Spit here."

Didn't he care about Seb? wondered Tim. He knew that Anne had phoned him but surely he would be anxious about recent developments. Maybe the old fool had forgotten his existence. They walked into the lounge. Now they could see the man's face. He was quite young – in his late twenties – and clean-shaven. His complexion was pinkish and there was an earnestness in his manner that was offputting. So were his eyes. They were a kind of slate blue, cold and disinterested.

"This is Mr Watson from the power station," said Teddy, as if he was introducing royalty. Obviously he was very proud to be visited by someone from Sea Spit, however hard he had campaigned against his interests. "Flower, Brian and Tim – all members of Green Watch."

Philip Watson rose from his cramped position and shook their hands. "How is your father?" he asked immediately.

"He's going to be OK," Flower replied, flatly.

"Appalling accident – hit and run driver, I gather."

"Yes."

"He was en route to see me."

"Yes." Her voice was still flat, without expression, and there was an awkward silence.

"Is he conscious?" Philip Watson said suddenly.

"Yes, he's conscious."

"Do they – have they caught the—"

"No," said Flower, still acting as spokesperson. "They haven't caught anybody."

"I'm very sorry."

"My stepmother's with him now."

"I do hope he'll recover without – recover quickly."

The conversation died a horrible death and there was a good deal of throat clearing. Tim was plucking up courage to ask about the Reapers when Flower pre-empted him.

"Has Mr Cormack told you why my father was coming to see you this morning?"

"No. He was – er – telling me about – certain phenomena—"

"And the Reapers?"

"Quite a sinister nickname. The group of men on the beach." His voice was jovial, almost hearty.

"That was what he was coming to see you about."

19

"Oh yes?"

"He wanted to know what was going on."

"The fishermen? I can quite easily explain that." He laughed. "It's something in the nature of a treasure hunt."

"Treasure hunt?" said Flower disbelievingly.

"Yes. You see I heard about the Reapers, as you imaginatively call them, a while back. They'd been on the beach for about a week then. So I went to a fisherman I knew, and eventually I was told – perhaps reluctantly, for I believe they feel rather foolish."

"Why should they?" asked Brian suspiciously.

"Well, it sounds stupid, but one of their wives lost a diamond-studded gold watch—"

"Wouldn't it be easier to look for it in the day?" snapped Tim sarcastically.

"I haven't finished," said Watson patiently. "They searched thoroughly in daylight but the watch is very small and they had no luck. But it has a luminous dial which shines out in the dark so they thought they might be more successful at night. It's valuable – both financially and sentimentally. Hence the search."

"And they haven't found anything yet?" asked Brian.

"No. I personally don't think they will."

"How long do you reckon they'll go on searching?"

"They might give it another couple of nights."

This is incredible, thought Tim. Does he think we're complete idiots? What a ridiculous story. "But why do they do it so late? They could do it directly it gets dark."

"That's the point." Watson smiled smugly. "It's a surprise for Edie."

"Edie?" The whole story was getting more and more bizarre, thought Tim.

"The wife. She's only nineteen. And heart-broken about losing the watch."

"Do you seriously expect us to believe this?" demanded Flower.

"Well, young lady," Watson began with insufferable patronage, "there have been stranger things than this, you know." He laughed. "But they're not looking for monsters on the beach as your father suggested. That I can assure you. And I want you to assure me of something—"

Tim had a horrible sensation of being trapped in a web of almost reasonable lies and wondered if the others were feeling the same.

"There *have* been two unfortunate incidents at Sea Spit, but they presented no threat at all to the general public. And there is no queston of them occurring again." He smiled at Teddy. "I can quite understand how these fears are taken up by the locals, but they're really groundless."

"Are you a public relations man?" asked Brian. Only Flower and Tim could detect the very slight sneer in his voice.

"Well," Watson's voice was light, casual, reasonable, "I wouldn't put it like that."

"How *would* you put it?"

"I'm a communications officer. Too many people think we keep secrets at Sea Spit. My aim is to tell the truth – that we don't."

Brian turned to the silent Teddy. "What do you think? Does his explanation satisfy you?"

The old man shook his head. "Beats me."

"It's not easy," began Watson, "living under the shadow of local rumour. Now—"

Teddy went on as if he hadn't heard him. "Beats me," he repeated.

"What does?" asked Flower gently.

"I don't know about them Reapers – maybe the gentleman's right. But I saw them with my very own eyes."

"Saw what exactly?" said Watson.

"The monsters," Teddy said. "The monsters on the beach."

Tim darted a glance at Watson. For a few brief seconds his smug patronage had slipped away. On his face was a look of acute anxiety.

Watson left a few minutes later in a whirl of reassuring comments, which included "easy enough to see things at night" and "total reassurance that Sea Spit is one hundred per cent safe" and "the very best of luck to Mr Howard". When he had gone, Flower turned to Teddy sternly.

"Listen—"

"What are you on about now?" he muttered, tired and ruffled.

"I want you to tell us what you *really* saw."

"Don't you believe me?" Teddy asked aggressively.

"Yes," said Flower softly. "But we want to hear all about it again."

"You *don't* believe me."

"Please, Teddy—"

"I already told you. I seen big crabs by the tideline. Scurrying about like. And I saw big sea cabbages. Twice the normal size. Maybe three times."

"When did you see them? Once? Twice?"

"I saw 'em one night. Couldn't sleep. Then – in the morning they were gone."

It all sounded even more doubtful than ever, thought Tim. Just an old man's dream. No wonder Seb had been sceptical.

"You want some cocoa?" asked Teddy pathetically, still knowing that no one believed him but with all his aggression gone.

"I'm going to ring the hospital," said Flower, ignoring him.

Teddy said very little for the rest of the evening, squatting in front of his televison set, hardly moving – an old husk of a man, lonely and disbelieved. There was little news from the hospital and although Anne rang twice, saying that Seb was sleeping, the official view was "comfortable".

The three of them sat round and played cards, not concentrating hard enough to give the game any edge. Then, slowly, aimlessly, and one by one, they went to bed, muttering subdued goodnights to the hunched figure of Teddy.

Chapter Three

"Tim!"

"What?"

"Come on, Tim."

"Wassamatter?"

"I want to show you, Tim – show you things you never dreamed of." Tim opened his eyes to find Teddy beside him, whisky on his breath.

"What's the time?"

"Nigh on three."

"You barmy?"

"Not so as you'd notice." The old man chuckled. "Them Howards think I am."

"What do you want?"

"Come with me. I want to prove it to you."

"Prove what?"

"There's monsters on the beach."

"Oh, Teddy—"

"Just let me show you."

Tim groaned. It had been his turn to sleep on the sofa. The others were down the corridor, sleeping without interruption. He wished he was.

"Look, Teddy—"

"Please." There was a note of urgency in the old man's voice now. "Please, Tim."

"All right." He tumbled off the sofa and began to search for his jeans. "You'd better have something to show me."

The night was very still and the dark waves lapped idly at the beach.

"What about the Reapers?" asked Tim.

"Not abroad tonight."

"You sure?"

"Been waiting up, haven't I?"

"Where're we going?"

"Up a pace."

"What's that mean?"

"Past the drying sheds – up to Sea Spit."

"Can't we walk on the road? It's easier," complained Tim.

"Best stick to the beach. I seen it up there."

"It?"

"Wriggling about like."

"Teddy —"

"Come on."

26

"You been out?"

"Sure I been out. That's when I saw it. The beast. Wriggling along."

Tim followed him gloomily as he stumped over the pebbles. He was sure that whatever Teddy had seen had a good deal to do with the whisky he had been drinking.

"There."

"Where?" asked Tim critically.

"There. You got eyes, haven't you?"

There was a slight indentation in the pebble ridge, as if someone had dragged something along it. That was all.

"So what?"

"So everything. This is where the beast was."

"What kind of beast?"

"Slimy great thing. Kind of sea snake."

The waves murmured at the tideline, sighing as they occasionally swamped the pebbles.

"Teddy—"

"Don't you believe me?" He was suddenly aggressive.

"Well—"

"Then I saw one of them crabs. The monster crabs." He spoke quickly, almost frantically. There was something pathetic about him now, as he tried desperately to convince Tim.

"Oh yes?"

"Down by the shore. The snake got at it."

"It did?"

"I can prove it – look—" He stumbled towards the sea and Tim followed reluctantly. Great waves of tiredness kept sweeping over him. How could Teddy be so selfish? What with Seb so desperately ill and—

"See?"

"What?"

"Am I lying? Now?"

"Blimey!" Tim was staring at something half buried in the pebbles. It was a monster claw.

"Go on – touch it then. Do you think it's made of wood? That it's a fake?"

Tim picked it up gingerly. The claw was wet and clammy and there was something soft at the end of it. He dropped it with a little cry.

"Real?"

"Well—"

"Torn off, you see."

"By the—"

"Snake. Ripped off."

"Yes—" Tim stared down at it doubtfully, feeling slightly nauseated.

Teddy looked towards the dark shape of Sea Spit Nuclear Power Station, looming immediately above them. "You mark my words, they're making monsters."

"Wait—"

"What's up?"

"There's something coming out of the power station," said Tim, screwing up his eyes and trying to pick it out more clearly in the moonlight. "It looks like – like a rat."

"Mighty big for a rat," replied Teddy.

Whatever it was paused and looked out into the wind. It certainly wasn't a dog, thought Tim, nor a cat or a fox. But Teddy was right – it was very big for a rat. Far too big. So it couldn't be a rat, he told himself. Could it? The thing seemed to whiffle at the air – then bound into the night.

"What did I tell you?" whispered Teddy.

Tim bent down and picked up the claw. "We need this," he said, recoiling as his fingers closed on its damp softness. Even the scaly hardness was horrible to the touch. "As evidence."

Tim slept very badly the rest of the night. He dreamt wild impossible dreams of the rat-like creature bounding down the pebbles from Sea Spit and clambering through one of the windows of the railway carriage. It curled up beside him in his bed, and when in his dream he awoke, it was licking his throat, baring its huge yellow teeth, its eyes burning into him like fire. Then he really woke up, sweating and shivering at the same time. Somehow he drifted back into uneasy sleep again and this time he dreamt of Philip Watson, walking the midnight beach, the rat thing straining at a leash. He was striding towards the railway carriage, almost being dragged along by his slavering companion.

"Wake up, Tim."

"Mm?"

"Wake up."

"It's coming."

"What?"

"It's coming down here." Tim opened his eyes to see Brian with a cup of tea in his hand.

"What's up?"

"What? Wassamatter?"

"Your bedclothes are all on the floor. Been having a nightmare?"

"Something like that."

"You look lousy."

"Thanks."

"Drink this."

Tim sipped at the tea gratefully. "I was out last night."

"Why?"

"Teddy took me."

"Oh did he?" Brian looked at him suspiciously.

Tim burst into a stumbling explanation, ending in the sighting of the rat thing, then got out of bed to retrieve the claw which he had put in the bottom of a rickety cupboard. Brian picked it up and sighed. It looked odd in the morning light.

"I wondered when he'd try this."

Flower came in and, taking one look at the claw, started to giggle. "So he caught you," she said.

"What do you mean?"

"Maybe we should have warned you." Brian shrugged. "But what with Dad and everything—"

"What the hell are you on about?" snapped Tim.

"I spotted him rooting about in the kitchen last

night, so I kept an eye on him from the door."

"You mean you spied on him?"

"With good reason," said Brian indignantly.

"He's been stirring it up." Flower spoke sadly, and even through his anger Tim knew how much she cared for the old man.

"Well?"

"He's got another one of these."

"*What?*"

"Probably going to hide it somewhere else on the beach tonight."

"But—"

"It's made of balsa wood, I think," said Brian. "Painted and with this gooey stuff shoved in the torn-off end. It's hardened up. Probably fibre glass."

Tim grabbed the claw and examined it. There was a smell of the sea but underneath something else. Something chemical. He met Flower's eyes reluctantly.

"So he made it?"

"Want to check the kitchen cupboard? He's still asleep."

Tim shook his head. "I'll take your word for it," he said. "But why does he do it?"

"I suppose he's so anxious about Sea Spit – he's so convinced that it's doing harm – that he felt if there wasn't enough evidence then he'd better make it up." Flower spoke slowly. "After all, apart from the Reapers – and there may even be an explanation of a kind for them – there's nothing, is there?"

Tim thought of the rat thing – and what about the

marks where something had been dragged over the pebbles? But what did they really mean? One could have been a trick of the light; the other nothing at all. He just didn't want to say anything to the others. Suddenly he thought of something else. "Why did he try and fool *me*, then? And not you two?"

There was a long awkward pause. Then Brian said, "I think he just wanted to jerk us all into action. He really *believes* something is going on – and I'm sure he's right."

"He thinks the Howard family don't believe a word he says," Flower put in quickly. "So he'd try it out on someone a bit less cynical."

She's good at face-saving, thought Tim. So he decided to risk being scoffed at and explained to them all about the horrors of seeing the rat thing. "What could it have been?" He tailed off, wondering if they were going to laugh at him.

But Brian only shrugged. "Sure it wasn't a dog?"

"Sure."

"Look," Flower was suddenly quite fierce, "we've got to thrash this out, once and for all. Do we think there's something going on at Sea Spit or not?"

Again there was a long silence. Then Brian said, "Dad doesn't think there's much in it."

"Dad doesn't know everything," said Flower sharply. "And what about the accident?"

"It was an accident," said Brian. "Just that."

"It seems an odd coincidence." Tim was hesitant. "We come down here to investigate Teddy's story, see the Reapers, get a funny explanation – and then

Seb's in this hit and run—" Tim stopped in mid-flow, suddenly panicky with guilt. "I didn't ask how he is. Have you phoned—"

"He's making progress," said Flower shortly. "Go on."

"Nothing else to say. It just seems weird; even if I didn't see a monster rat, even if dear old Teddy tried to fabricate the evidence."

"I tell you what we should do." Brian's voice was urgent with new decisiveness. "We should confront him."

"Teddy?"

"Make him tell us what's true and what's not."

"OK," replied Flower doubtfully. "Let's give it a swing."

"Teddy?"

"What do you want?"

"Tea?"

"All right."

They had all crowded into the small kitchen with Tim elected spokesperson on the grounds that he was not a member of the doubting Howards.

Teddy was sitting at the table looking despondent, his gnarled hands clasped together and his head down. Tim passed him the tea and he stared at it miserably.

"Come clean." Tim plunged in desperately. "This claw – you made it, didn't you?"

He raised rheumy eyes and a stained beard to Tim.

There were tears in his eyes and Tim felt a rush of compassion for him and knew the others were feeling the same.

"No."

"No?"

"That was from a monster, that claw—"

"It's made of wood and fibre glass," said Tim patiently. "*You* made it and there's another one in the kitchen cupboard."

"You saw that—"

"I thought I saw some kind of huge rat. But now I've thought about it again I know it was a trick of the light."

"Yeah—"

"Well, Teddy?" asked Flower gently. "What about it?"

"All right – it's a fair cop." He looked up ruefully. "I was only trying to get you to believe me." He got up slowly, walked to a cupboard and brought out an identical claw. Now that Tim knew it was a fake it looked totally ridiculous. Teddy snapped it in half and threw the remains on the floor. "So I've been a damn fool."

"Why are you so desperate?" asked Flower in the same gentle voice.

"I know they're covering up something," he said grimly. "That radiation leak did something to this strip of beach, and it did something to me."

"To you?" asked Brian incredulously.

"My hair's falling out, and I've had this terrible rash on my hands. It comes and goes, but it's back now with a vengeance." He held out the backs of his wrists. Sure enough there was an angry red rash there.

"Have you been to the doctor?" began Flower. "I mean, if you—"

"I don't hold with doctors. I know they've done something up there. Something they're hushing up."

"But how do you *know*? Have you really seen monsters on the beach?" rapped out Brian.

"I seen that rat thing, and there's been these big sea cabbages—"

"So why did you make the claws?"

"Because no one was listening to me. Your dad was walking out – until they ran him down."

"We don't know that," said Tim. "It could just be an ordinary accident."

"They think he knows more than he's letting on."

"Who's they?"

"Those freaks at Sea Spit."

Tim sighed. They were getting nowhere. It all seemed like an old man's fantasy now. Maybe even Watson's peculiar explanation about the Reapers was right. They might as well pack up and go home – it was all so frustrating.

"You're going home then?" Teddy sounded matter-of-fact.

"We have to go back to school next week," said Flower. "And it's Thursday already. Of course Dad's going to be in hospital for some time."

"You go," he said, standing up. But there was no hostility in his voice – just acceptance.

"We'll stay until the weekend," said Brian. "But we've got to go and see Dad now, OK?"

"You'll be welcome," said Teddy flatly. "Welcome to stay."

"Where are you going?" asked Tim.

"Walking the beach," he said. "It's my world, see?"

They all looked at him in concern. Teddy seemed utterly defeated.

"Dad?"

"Mm."

"How you feeling?"

"Mm."

Seb lay on the bed in a small side ward. At least he'd been moved out of intensive care. Nevertheless he seemed to have just as many tubes and dials about him. Anne sat beside him, hollow-eyed and exhausted.

"He won't say much to you," she said, "but he's making progress."

They sat and told her about Teddy – what they had said to him, and what they had decided to do. At the end of their explanation she said, "I'm sure you've all done the right thing. There's no point in going on—" But just as she was finishing the sentence Seb began to groan, and then to whisper. Anne reached out for his hand. "It's all right," she said. "It's all right." Seb however did not calm down at all. Instead, he seemed to become more agitated than before.

"What's the matter with him?' asked Flower fearfully.

"He's seems to be trying to say something." Anne gently pushed Seb back. He continued to mutter indistinctly. Then his voice became clearer.

"Don't – give – up."

"Why?' asked Anne softly. "Why, Seb?"

"Don't—"

"Why?" she repeated.

"I'm sure – it's – they – forced – me – off—"

"They?"

"Who?" demanded Brian but Anne raised a hand to subdue him.

"They?" she repeated. "Who are *they*, Seb?"

But he started muttering again – and then he slept.

"They—" repeated Flower. "Does he mean Sea Spit? And not to give up. If only he knew how much Teddy has been lying." Her voice tailed away. "They – who are *they*?"

"Where is he?"

"Probably still wandering about the beach."

It was late afternoon and warm, mellow sunshine filtered through the pebbles. Everything was very clear and the sea was still, hardly moving, its surface scummy and greasy looking. Sea Spit stood out starkly in the hard light.

"Can't see him." They were standing by the

railway carriage, vaguely uneasy.

"There's something floating out there - look! in the shallows," said Flower suddenly.

They all began to run towards the sea.

Chapter Four

The figure was face down in the listless water.

"Who is it?" yelled Tim. They were all running as fast as they could through the shallows, Brian a few metres in front.

"It's Teddy!"

"Get him in!"

"He's dead!"

"Get him in!"

The three of them dragged and propelled him in. Then, pulling him up on to the pebbles, Brian began to apply artificial respiration, alternately pressing down on the old man's chest and breathing into his mouth in a steady rhythm. For a long while there was no response until, quite suddenly, he began to splutter out water.

"Turn him over and see if he can breathe," said Flower.

Brian carefully rolled him sideways and more water drained out of Teddy's lungs. He groaned and choked but he was breathing all right.

"What's that?"

Faintly they could hear the staccato sound of a motor boat engine.

"I thought I saw something," said Brian. "As I was running out into the water. A dark shape. Behind those rocks. Right over there. But I wasn't looking, I was only concentrating on Teddy."

"Was he in it?" Tim stared down at Teddy.

"No time to ask now," snapped Flower. "We need an ambulance."

It was while they were waiting for the ambulance that they spotted the upturned boat behind a breakwater.

"So he was in that. Nothing to do with the motor boat," said Flower. But she was interrupted by the siren of the ambulance and the accompanying police car.

It could well have everything to do with that motor boat, thought Tim.

"Looks as if the old boy capsized in his rowing boat," said the policeman when the ambulance had taken Teddy away.

"What about the motor boat?" asked Brian.

"I don't see how any other boat could have been involved," he said. They were standing over the rowing boat which together they had managed to right. "There isn't a mark on it. The tide just nudged it up on to the beach."

"We're not even sure if it's his boat. We never knew he *had* a boat," insisted Flower. "He said he was going for a walk."

The policeman wasn't impressed. "He's a bit of a character, isn't he? I mean, I've met him before. Bit eccentric like." He paused self-consciously. "Related to him, are you?"

Flower shook her head. "Just good friends," she replied sarcastically.

Teddy was taken to the same hospital as Seb but he didn't go into intensive care. Instead, he was settled into a small room at the end of the ward.

"I'm getting used to this place," said Brian, as they waited for a nurse to give them some information.

"I just don't get it." Tim was upset and mystified. "First Seb and now him. It's as if someone's trying to pick them off."

"He must know something," said Brian. "Something that they thought Dad knew. And didn't."

"Teddy *knows* something?" Flower was scornful. "He's spent all his time lying. How could he know anything? He'd have told us soon enough."

"Maybe he doesn't *know* what he knows," hazarded Tim. "That's always a possibility."

41

They fell silent, wondering what to do. This was the first time Green Watch had had an unseen enemy, thought Tim. In their three previous adventures, their adversaries had had names, motives. But in this case, there was nothing. Only a grim threat that had left them without any adults around them at all, with Seb and Teddy suffering in this building and Anne now moving between them both, for Flower had contacted her directly they arrived at the hospital and briefed her on everything.

Tim looked covertly at Brian and Flower. They don't seem like kids any more, he thought. They had all taken on so much responsibility in the service of Green Watch over the last year – badgers, whales, dolphins, and now some unseen pollution that might not even exist at all. And yet with Seb nearly killed in the Landrover and Teddy nearly drowned, what were they to think? He looked again at his friends: Brian with his bookish ways and sudden spurts of relentless action; Flower more resolute and tough than she had ever been, yet looking so beautiful and somehow childish with her scruffy old jeans and tangled fair hair. He felt a stab of real fear. What would he do if anything happened to her or Brian? His life would be over. He couldn't bear it without them – not after all they had shared. They were all so close, and now so alone, maybe facing the worst, most powerful danger of all. Something unseen. Something terrible.

"It's up to us now," said Flower suddenly, as if she had guessed his thoughts.

"We can't chicken out now," he agreed.

"Chicken out of what?" asked Brian impatiently.

Just then the nurse came up. She was young and friendly.

"Are you family?" she asked.

"As good as," said Tim. "He hasn't got any real family."

"OK. Well, he's a tough old gentleman. He's going to get better."

"Great." There were tears in Flower's eyes, and Tim could feel them pricking at his own.

"But he'll need to be in here for a few days. Just to make sure he doesn't catch pneumonia or anything."

Anne arrived before they could ask to see him and as she did so, the nurse slipped away.

"How's Dad?" asked Brian.

"Still not saying much – just mumbling. But the doctor is happy with him. I gather Teddy's going to be all right. I've just seen one of the nurses."

"It's all weird," said Flower. "Don't you agree?"

"I don't know what to think." Anne looked incredibly tired. "But I don't want you going back to that railway carriage."

"That's just what we've got to do," said Flower very firmly and Tim smiled. He'd known all along she was going to make the decision. "That's what Dad managed to say – we mustn't give up."

"Yes, but—" Anne's voice tailed off.

"You're a member of Green Watch now," said Brian. "You know we've got to see it through."

"If only I understood what was going on," she said uneasily.

"That's what we're all wondering," agreed Brian. "Hints - that's all we've got to go on."

"But Teddy *must* have known something," said Tim. "Though why on earth he didn't tell us instead of making up all that stuff—"

"Well, you can't see him," put in Anne. "I've just tried. They won't let anyone in. He's to have complete rest."

"So we're stuck," muttered Tim.

"Are we?" Flower had the light of battle in her eyes. "I'm going to search that old wreck of a railway carriage till I find something."

"For God's sake!" said Anne. "I don't *want* you in there."

"But we'll have to be, won't we?" Flower put a hand on her arm. "We'll have to be. For both their sakes."

They arrived back on the beach at about nine o'clock, not sure whether to be grateful for the warm, still mantle of darkness or not. When they had made some food, which they ate ravenously, they divided up the railway carrige into three roughly equal sections and began to search. It was a draining business - Teddy seemed to have accumulated so many things. There were trunks and bulging drawers of papers, newspaper cuttings, old army records, letters from someone who appeared to have once been his wife, letters from someone else who seemed to have had wifely status at the same time, letters from other women, romantically written, bills, laundry tickets – he had kept everything. But nothing even remotely connected with Sea Spit turned up at all. At midnight they were exhausted and bad tempered but there were still more drawers, boxes and trunks of papers to be scrutinised.

Then Tim found something. At first, dazed by the mounds of paper and documents, he almost put it down. Then he read it again, and shouted for Flower and Brian.

"What is it?" asked Flower.

"Look at this." He held up the newspaper cutting.

"Blimey!"

PROTESTER GETS SIX YEARS

A young protester who gained access to Sea Spit Nuclear Power Station received a six-year prison sentence for causing thousands of pounds worth of damage as he wreaked havoc with an axe.

Disguised as a worker, with a stolen pass, 22-year-old Steven Cormack kept security men at bay for nearly two hours as he locked himself in a top security area of the reactor, kidnapping 50-year-old process worker Adam Jameson and causing him grievous bodily harm. Although psychiatric reports recommended hospital treatment the judge, Justice Bernard Waterman, imposed the prison sentence.

Asked if he had anything to say, Cormack claimed that a strip of beach had been enclosed by Sea Spit because it was heavily contaminated with radiation and that there had been an alteration to its character. A representative of the nuclear power station later told me that there was no question of any contaminated beach being enclosed.

Clipped to the cutting were a pile of letters. Some of them were from a prison, the rest from a psychiatric hospital. The cutting was dated February 12th, 1981. The last letter was dated July 18th, 1988, two years previously. They thumbed through the letters, passing them from one to another. They were sad, talking about prison conditions, asking for parcels, demanding a campaign for parole. One indicated that he was being sent to the hospital but the letters from there didn't change much, and were still preoccupied with the same matters as the ones from prison – conditions, parcels and parole. But the most revealing thing was the fact that every letter ended: "*With much love, Steve*" and began "*Dear Dad.*"

"So he's got a son!" said Flower, and Tim smiled. Flower was usually such a quick thinker. She must be totally exhausted to state the obvious like that.

"He had plenty of women," pointed out Brian. "I'm surprised he didn't have more children."

"Maybe he did," said Tim. "But this explains a lot, doesn't it? His son breaks in—"

"Storms in," suggested Flower.

"Creates havoc, takes a man hostage. I'm amazed Dad didn't know about this. Why didn't Teddy say something?" mused Brian.

46

"Maybe he's ashamed his son's in a mental hospital," said Flower. "Or maybe – maybe they're keeping him there," she speculated.

"Who?" asked Brian.

"I don't know – the authorities—" she finished lamely.

"That's a bit far-fetched, isn't it?"

"I don't know," said Tim. "Depends what he found out." He shuddered. "I don't like the idea of that private beach much. Do you?"

They didn't.

"What shall we do?" asked Flower.

But Brian wasn't listening. "Maybe," he said, "just maybe this is what Teddy's been keeping quiet about. Maybe he was afraid to bring Steve into it, or mention him, so all he felt he could do was to stir it up with a few pathetic props, hoping we'd follow his false trail and find some real leads by chance."

"He called us in," began Flower.

"But gave us none of the right information – too scared to," Brian repeated. "So we've only got two prongs of attack."

"Which are?" asked Tim fearfully.

"First, get to see Steve."

"But he'd be released by now," said Tim, looking at the date.

"I'd like to check that."

"How?"

"By ringing the hospital," said Brian relentlessly. "After all, Teddy's nearly been killed. Isn't that compassionate grounds?"

"For releasing him?" asked Flower doubtfully.

"No, for contacting him."

"And supposing he's being held?" asked Tim.

"All this 'being held'!" said Flower. "It sounds as if we're up against the government."

"Maybe we are," replied Brian quietly. "It's not going to be easy to get to see him. But we've got to."

"And the other prong?" asked Flower.

"Get into Sea Spit."

"Impossible!"

"I shan't be carrying an axe," said Brian sarcastically. "I'll be more discreet than Steve."

"Why you?" demanded Flower.

"We can't all go."

"We can. Either all three of us, or no one."

"We haven't asked Tim's opinion," said Brian slowly.

"If we get caught," said Tim, "we've had it. And I've been in trouble for breaking in before."*

"Sure—"

"But—"

"But what, Tim?"

"There's a lot at stake, isn't there?"

"A damn sight more than ever before. This is a really serious environmental issue, with long-lasting effects. Green Watch must be able to handle it."

Tim thought of that beach again – desolate and enclosed. Were there monsters there? He remembered that the walls of Sea Spit ran right down

* *Dolphin's Revenge*

48

to the sea; it was almost as impregnable as a castle. What were they doing? Polluting the landscape and keeping a young man prisoner? He felt a terrible rage growing inside him. He thought of his own father, still in prison. He had committed a crime and would soon be freed. And Seb had even offered to take him on a Green Watch adventure. Maybe give him a job, if he wanted it. But Steve, this stranger, he should have served his sentence, but maybe they hadn't let him go. Maybe they'd keep him there forever. And also – had they tried to kill Seb? And Teddy? Because of what they knew, or what these secret people thought they knew?

"I'm with you," he said decisively. "Whatever the risks."

"Great!" said Brian and Flower smiled. The smile made Tim more elated than he had felt in months.

"What's the plan then?" asked Tim.

They were all very tired. It was really late now and the night had remained still and quiet.

"Tomorrow I'll go and see Anne," Brian said. "Tell her what we've discovered and get her to ring this psychiatric hospital – Viewforth."

"OK."

"While I'm with her, you two go and have a look at Sea Spit."

"Inside?" gasped Tim.

"Outside, you prat! See what security's like. It should be very tight. But maybe from the sea—"

"Perhaps that's where Teddy was trying from," said Flower suddenly.

"Maybe." Brian was too intent on the planning to dwell on him. "Just keep looking."

"Won't they be suspicious?"

"Not if you're casual."

"Casual?" asked Flower. "Sussing out a nuclear power station casually. I'd like to see you try!"

Brian grinned. "Just be kids. Playing around."

"Tag?" asked Tim. "Amongst the reactors?"

"How about bikes outside?"

"Bikes?"

"Teddy's got two ancient ones in the shed."

"So he has," said Flower. "I wonder if one of them was ever Steve's?"

"Just ride them about," said Brian quickly. "Any other questions? I'm knackered."

They went to bed, tired, hardly believing in what they were about to do. At least that's what Tim felt. But almost immediately he was in the deep, dreamless sleep of utter exhaustion. From the very depths of this he surfaced to an insistent tapping on his shoulder.

"What? Who? What?"

"It's Flower."

"What—"

"Someone's knocking."

"Where?"

"On the door, you idiot!"

"Where's Brian?"

"I'm here."

"What do we do?"

"Open it," said Brian resolutely. "That's the usual thing to do."

"What about doing nothing?" suggested Tim.

"If they want to get in, one foot on that rotten wood would be enough."

"All right," said Tim. "Let's open the door."

Flower opened the door. The night was warm, scented with tar and seaweed and brine. In front of them stood a stocky middle-aged man in a blue sweater, corduroy trousers and gum-boots. He wore horn-rimmed glasses which made his wide, tanned face look almost school-masterly.

"What do you want?" asked Flower. "Do you know how late it is?"

"I know that right enough." His voice was soft and slightly mocking.

"Well, didn't it occur to you that social visits—"

"And I have something to tell you," he continued, ignoring her sarcasm.

"Wat is it?" asked Brian. "What is it that can't wait till tomorrow?"

"It's a warning."

A chill settled in Tim's stomach.

"Well?" Flower didn't sound surprised.

"You lot are meddling in things you shouldn't. You'd best clear off."

"Now?" Her voice was icy.

"As soon as possible."

"Are you a Reaper?" asked Brian.

"A what?"

"One of the gang that prowl up and down the beach at night." His voice was as icy as Flower's. If only I could feel as cool, thought Tim. Instead of being so scared. He could see the man's eyes behind his glasses in the moonlight. They were like darting tadpoles.

"I don't know what you're on about."

"No?"

"What I do know – what I'm telling you – is to clear off out of it."

"And if we don't?"

"You'll suffer the consequence that busybodies should suffer."

Tim shivered. The man had a strong accent and his voice sounded homely and threatening at the same time. It wasn't a pleasant combination.

"We're staying," said Flower. "We're on holiday."

The man smiled sourly. "You're nosing about."

"Go away," she said. "Or I'll call the police."

"I'm giving you a warning," the man said again.

"Get out!" She slammed the door in his face and they waited behind it tremulously, wondering if he would break it down. But after a few seconds they heard his heavy tread on the pebbles. It seemed to go on for ages.

"What are we going to do?" asked Tim.

"Carry on as usual," said Brian.

Chapter Five

The next morning they were rather subdued. The man had been very sure of himself, and his presence hung like a threat in the air. Even Flower looked nervous.

"The plan's the same," she said, turning to Brian. "Isn't it?"

He nodded. "I'm going to the hospital. You take a look at Sea Spit. Be childish – cycle around – look immature." They would have joked about that before last night's visit.

"Listen," said Flower. "I don't know what we're up against, but whatever it is it's big and powerful and it's got a lot to lose. Remember Dad and Teddy—" Her voice broke. "They've already suffered enough. We've got to be careful."

"Yes," replied Brian. He took her hand. "Don't worry, Flower. We'll all walk up to the bus stop together, and then I'll be with loads of people in town. It's you two who've got to be careful."

Not for the first time since he had joined Green Watch, Tim wanted to be back at home with his mother and far away from the unseen, unknown enemy that faced them here.

Tim and Flower waited until Brian's bus came before they left him. Then, steadying the old cycles they had found in the shed, they stood by the roadside, watching the small country bus trundle off into the distance. Tim looked round nervously.

"It's weird – I feel we're being watched all the time."

"Don't say that, Tim." Flower laughed. "It sounds as if you're going off your trolley."

"Maybe I am."

"No, I have to admit I feel the same as you. What's happened has made even the ordinary seem sinister. Know what I mean?"

"Yes," said Tim gloomily. "I know exactly what you mean."

They got on their bikes and pedalled stiffly along the flat road back to Sea Spit. The sky was overcast and a light drizzle began to descend on them as they approached the gates of the power station. There was a security checkpoint at the front and a high wire fence surrounding the actual building itself. It looked impenetrable. They stared at it hopelessly. How naive they had been to think they could ever get in.

"We're just kids," muttered Flower.

"Eh?"

"Silly kids with big ideas."

"Why do you say that?"

"Look at the place. There's no way in there. No way at all."

"No?"

"Look at it."

"Look at *that*!" said Tim triumphantly.

"What?"

"The truck. The delivery truck."

"That provisions thing?"

"It's local."

"So—"

"It means we could get in it."

"Even if we could," said Flower doubtfully, "they'd discover us in no time."

"Not if one of us was in a box."

"What?"

"A box marked – I don't know, 'Extra potatoes, do not open' or something."

"You're barmy!"

"Thanks." Tim was downcast.

"Even if we could find a box like that, how could we get it in the van? I mean, they'd know they hadn't ordered it. I tell you, we're just silly kids."

"No."

"We *are*."

He had never seen her so defeated. Tim searched

his mind desperately. Somehow he had to come up with something to restore her confidence.

"Wait—"

"Well?" she asked challengingly.

"Supposing we didn't get in the *provisions* van."

"Yeah?"

"But we got in one of *their* vans."

"How?" she asked unhelpfully.

"They must load up with things."

"We'd just be discovered, Tim. Haven't you got that through your head yet?"

He was silent for a long time. Then he said, "Teddy must've been trying to sail in there."

"Like the idiot he is."

"Maybe. But hasn't Seb got the diving equipment anywhere?"

"It's back at the Windmill – back at Romney."

Again Tim was silent, desperately racking his brains, feeling more and more helpless in the face of her negative attitude.

Then Flower said quickly: "Got it!"

"What?"

"I've got it. Thanks for coming up with so many ideas."

"They were all useless."

"But they made me think. How about this —?" She pointed towards the entrance of Sea Spit. About a dozen drums were standing in a loading bay.

"They're full of something," said Tim.

"No they're not. I've just seen one of those men

56

rolling one down the ramp. And they've got a lid that screws on."

"So what do we do? The security guard's on the gate."

"If one of us distracted him, the other could get into one of those drums. They're behind the security fence."

"And then?"

"And then you're inside."

Tim considered. "It's risky."

"Sure."

He considered again. "When?"

"We should try and get to see Steve first. He could help us. Then we do it."

"Who goes? It can't be all of us." He looked at her beseechingly.

"When the time comes we'll have to toss up," she said quietly. "All three of us." She looked at her watch. "Let's go and make some lunch. Brian might be back soon." There was an edge to her voice that Tim noticed immediately.

"He'll be all right."

"We're out of our depth here," she muttered.

Tim said nothing. There was no doubt that she was absolutely right.

Brian got back at about two to find them in an agony of suspense.

"Where the hell have you been?" asked Flower angrily.

57

"Travelling."

"All this time?"

"I came back as quickly—"

"What happened?" asked Tim anxiously.

"Dad's getting on pretty well." He spoke in a measured voice. "And Teddy's fine. No sign of pneumonia." He paused. "And Anne got through to Viewforth."

"Well?" Tim and Flower could hardly bear the suspense.

"She told them about Teddy—"

"You mean he's still there?"

"It was weird. She got through to a ward and they said he was there. Then someone cut in on the call. They said he wasn't."

"He wasn't *there*?" gasped Tim.

"That's what they said."

"What did Anne do?"

"Said she'd been told he was."

"And?"

"They said there'd been a mistake."

"Did she press it?"

"Sure. But they kept saying they didn't have a patient of that name. And that was that."

"Did she get the name of the ward?" rapped Flower. "From the original person, I mean."

"Yes. Baker Ward."

"So what are we going to do?"

"Anne's going to meet us there this afternoon."

Flower brightened up. "Great!"

"How we going to get in?"

"Just walk in – that's what she said – straight into Baker Ward."

Flower looked at him admiringly. "That's cool."

Tim thought it sounded downright dangerous. But nothing to what he and Flower had planned for Sea Spit.

"How did you get on?" asked Brian casually.

Flower began to tell him.

After lunch they set out on the bus to the hospital. Anne met them in the car park.

"Ready?"

"Sort of," said Tim.

"How's Dad?"

"We'll see him on the way back. Making real progress." Anne looked far less exhausted. "He's talking now, and the police have interviewed him. And as for Teddy, he's up and wandering round the ward."

"What if he tries to get out?" asked Brian.

"They've thought of that – they've taken away his clothes."

It was good to laugh, thought Tim. It put a temporary screen around what they had to do. But not for long, he thought, as he listened to Flower telling Anne about their plans.

"You can't *do* that!" she said when she had listened carefully to the barrel idea. She seemed horrified, particularly after Brian had told her about the warning. "I want you to get out of there. Come and

59

stay in a hotel here."

"No," said Flower determinedly.

"If your father knew—"

"He doesn't."

"I can't allow you to go on staying there, or climb into barrels at Sea Spit. You'd be arrested."

Or disposed of, thought Tim in his grimmest heart of hearts.

"We *must* go ahead! Dad would want us to," demanded Brian.

"Rubbish!" she said. But Tim knew that Seb Howard would probably let them take the risk.

The argument continued for a while until Anne exploded in exasperation.

"You *can't* do it!"

"We can."

Brian and Tim remained quiet. It seemed as if the argument had suddenly become personal between Flower and Anne, as if they were fighting some private battle for independence.

"I'll go to your—"

"How can you?"

"I can forbid you."

"How?"

"I'm your stepmother."

"You can't order us about." Flower was adamant, but she spoke quietly. She was much more controlled than Anne.

"It's so *foolhardy*!"

"It's necessary."

"What would Tim's parents say?"

"Don't know."

Tim remained silent. It still wasn't his argument. Then Flower said,

"Anne—"

"Well?" She sounded almost frightened.

"We're going. And there's nothing you can do to stop us."

"Then I won't take you to the hospital." Anne sounded almost childish now. "I would leave the decision to your father," she muttered, "but I don't want to worry him. It could really push back his recovery."

But Flower was insistent. "We'll go on our own."

"You won't get in."

"We'll just have to try."

"Flower—"

"No."

"Oh, God!" It was clear that Anne had lost. Now, quite suddenly, she seemed almost dependent on Flower.

"It'll be all right." Flower was gentle with her.

"No—"

"It'll be all right. Come on – let's go."

Flower marched towards the car park followed by Anne and the two boys. Tim knew Flower had won the battle.

Viewforth Psychiatric Hospital was composed of a forbidding Victorian central block surrounded by villas in woodland. They looked unkempt and slightly eerie. Reception had directed them to Baker Villa without any question.

"This is it," said Flower.

There was a vaguely Spanish look to it but crumbling stucco and peeling plaster gave it a desolate air.

"Flower—" began Anne.

"We're just going to walk in and ask for him," said Flower. "As you suggested," she added with a slight smile.

The villa smelt of stale food and stale lives. There didn't seem to be any staff around, but as they entered the foyer an old man tottered out in a dressing gown.

"We're looking for Steven Cormack," Anne said softly. "Do you know where he is?"

"Stevie?" The old man looked like an ancient wizened bird. He had a high, sing-song voice. "Stevie's around."

"Inside?"

"Oh no. Stevie doesn't like being inside."

"Then where—?"

"He'll be in the woods. Talking to his trees. He loves his trees."

"You mean – the wood behind the building?" Anne's voice was gentle.

"Just round there."

"What does he look like?" Tim knew she was taking a risk with her questions now, but the old man didn't seem in the least suspicious.

"You can't miss Stevie."

"No?"

"He looks like the prophet."

"Which prophet?"

"He's got long hair he has." He let out a shrill cackle of laughter and shuffled off down the drive.

"He's only got his dressing gown on," said Flower. "Shouldn't we tell someone?"

"I think he knows where he's going," said Brian. "Besides, if anyone official comes up, we could be out on our ear. Let's get to him. Now."

The woods behind the villa were deep and sombre, and the overcast sky of the morning seemed to have become lower and darker. The foliage was tangled and a single narrow path led through the trees. Brambles clawed at the trunks and there was a sharp smell of wild garlic.

"How long are we going on?" asked Flower. "Maybe he's not here after all."

Then, quite suddenly, they saw him. He was standing in a small clearing, staring up at an old oak tree which was wound round and half strangled by trails of ivy.

"Excuse me," said Anne softly.

Steven Cormack slowly turned round. He was very tall and thin, with tumbling yellow hair that fell onto his shoulders. His face was very striking, with high cheekbones, and he had pale blue eyes. But there was no serenity to him, only a kind of hopeless longing. Was he dangerous? wondered Tim. But there was something about the way he stood that was still and gentle.

"Are you Steve Cormack?"

"Yes."

"Your father's been taken ill. But he's going to be all right," said Anne in a very reassuring, calm, matter-of-fact tone.

There was no change of expression on Steven's face. "That's outside," he said.

"Outside?" Anne was puzzled.

"Outside life. It's not mine."

"Er – we came to talk to you."

"You can."

"But – do you want to?"

Steve looked back at the ivy-strangled oak. "I'm talking," he said.

"Will you talk to us?"

"I can't," he repeated. But he was still staring at the tree.

Tim felt a thrill of unease and when he looked at the others he could see they were very frightened. How could they get through to this walled-in man? And would he ever be able to understand what they were saying? Maybe he had forgotten the past, or didn't place any importance on it any more.

"Your father's been helping us," said Flower. "And we've been helping him. It's about Sea Spit."

Tim was amazed to see a total change come over

Steve. He looked as if someone had just punched him in the stomach.

"I don't know any more."

"We just—"

"You said I didn't know any more."

"What do you mean?" said Flower.

"You said that when you locked me up."

"We didn't lock you up."

"You said I was never to say – never to tell – never to have the chance—"

"We *didn't* lock you up."

He stared at them, as if he was trying to work something out.

"You're asking questions." Steve spoke very slowly.

"That's because we're friends of your father's," said Anne.

"What do you want?"

"We want to know about the beach – the polluted beach – the beach inside Sea Spit." Flower brought out the words in a panicky rush.

The result was incredible. A light of excitement seemed to fill Steve's wary china blue eyes and he stuttered slightly as he spoke. "It's there."

The fear left Tim and an unbearable excitement filled him.

Steve repeated the words. "It's there."

"You saw it?" asked Anne.

"That's why I'm here – that's why I'll always be here."

"No." Anne was very firm. "It's an injustice.

You're *not* always going to be here."

But he was adamant. "They'll make me stay."

They've driven him crazy, thought Tim. He was probably all right before. The hot anger filled him as he thought of his own father in prison, soon to be released. Suppose he'd been kept in forever? Just because he'd seen something he shouldn't.

"What did you see?" asked Flower.

"If I tell you—"

"We'll help you. They can't keep you here if it's all made public."

"Like in the papers?"

"Yes – and on the television."

His eyes lit up and there was a streak of sanity that was painful to see. "You mean – I could go away?"

"You could come home."

"How do I know I can trust you?" The wary gleam was back.

"You must," said Anne. "Your father's in hospital – you're stuck here. You *have* to trust us. Somehow."

He nodded, as if convinced of the fact. "All right."

"How did you get into Sea Spit?" asked Tim self-consciously.

"It was on a visit. They show parties round. I slipped away and put on a set of overalls I found in a cupboard. They missed me right away, but it took them a bit of time to find me. It's surprising how much ground you can cover in ten minutes." He laughed. "I wasn't very clever. Dad and I had always hated the place – it was an obscenity in that lovely spot, but worst of all we knew that there'd been a couple

66

of leaks and that it had all been hushed up. Then they started more building and took a whole stretch of beach into the compound. No one knew why – no one was told anything. So I was determined to have a look." He paused and his pale features seemed alive with anger again. "I managed to get right through the complex and ended up in a big room that had a plate glass window with a blind over it. There was a door and it said TOP SECURITY ONLY. I knew I didn't have much time. The room was completely bare except for a television screen which wasn't working. So I pulled up the blind." He paused again. "There was the beach."

There was complete stillness. A little wind rustled the ivy in the oak tree.

"Was it – different?" asked Brian.

Steve nodded. "It was amazing. There were huge sea cabbages all over it – about twice, maybe three times the size they should be. And there were other plants – all of them much bigger. They rose out of the pebbles like – like a forest. I just couldn't believe what I was looking at. And that wasn't all; there were things moving about amongst them."

"Things?"

"One looked like a giant cockroach; another a kind of worm. I didn't have much time to look at them. Someone came in and they started shouting. Then they pressed an alarm and the whole place was filled with the sound of a siren. I can't remember much more – I must have pushed past the man and the next thing I remember is finding myself in a store room. I took the axe and then grabbed somebody. I think we went into an office. Then all I can remember is the rage. The rage all the time." He stopped, exhausted. "I haven't talked about this for years. Not for years."

They were all stunned at what he had said. It was incredible, thought Tim. Could he be believed or not? Like his father, he had seen monsters on the beach. Tim remembered the rat thing and shuddered.

Chapter Six

"Will you get me out?" Steve asked as the wind again rustled the ivy.

"Do you want us to?" asked Anne suddenly.

"I don't know. I've grown used to it here. I love these trees – this wood."

"And the anger?"

"I don't feel anything – except for the trees."

"So—"

"I don't know if I want to come out. They'd never let me. Not now – after so long."

"Do you want—" But Anne was not to finish her sentence, for Steve had his finger to his lips.

"They're coming."

"They?"

"The nurses. You have to get away."

"We'll stay and talk to them," said Anne.

"You don't understand." Steve was very agitated now. "They'll hurt you—"

"Look—"

"Go. They'll hurt you."

Now they could hear people crashing through the undergrowth.

"Where do we go?" asked Flower.

"That way. Straight ahead. You'll get to a main road. It's busy."

"But we are—" said Anne.

"*Go!*"

He was so agitated now that they began to run. As they did so, a man in a white coat burst out of the bushes. He had a gun in his hand.

A shot cracked out as Steve hurled himself at the male nurse. The bullet whistled over Anne's head and hit a tree.

They ran on after a fleeting glimpse of Steve struggling on the ground with the nurse. Another shot was fired and again the bullet hit a tree. I don't believe this is happening! thought Tim as he tore down the path. I do believe this is happening, he assured himself as a thorny branch whipped his face. They ran on down the narrow path and the thickets grew more and more dense around them. Then, suddenly, it widened until they were up against a high wire fence – something that separated them from the busy main road, an obstacle that Steve had forgotten to warn them about.

Tim leapt for the meshed wire, tearing his

fingers but at least getting a grip on it. Straining every muscle he made it. On top was a flat piece, a kind of roll of wire. He lay on it while the others jumped for the mesh, heaved themselves up and climbed. One by one they grasped his hand, almost pulling him off in the process. Then, miraculously, they were all up there and starting to clamber down the other side. There was no immediate sign of pursuit and they wandered down the roadside and back towards the hospital car park, feeling shaky and exhausted.

"How weird!" said Flower. "Fancy carrying a gun."

"Maybe he's Steve's guard," volunteered Brian.

"You mean he could be – guarded all the time?" Anne sounded shocked.

"Guarded for the rest of his life?" mused Brian. "It's horrible!"

Once back in the normality of the hospital car park, they found it hard to believe that the incident had ever happened. All was calm, with rows of silent waiting cars, a sleepy attendant, a few people coming and going. The hospital directional signs were sombre and official, a nurse hurried across a paved square, telephones rang, a doctor walked briskly to a car. A man with a gun was unthinkable, impossible – a fantasy.

Anne opened the door of her battered Renault and they clambered in. She gave the withered attendant the ticket, he passed a rheumy eye over it and demanded money. She paid him and they drove out. It was ridiculous, thought Tim, as he looked back at the desolate greyness of the car park, to think of anything out of the ordinary happening here.

"We'll go straight back," said Anne. "I'll see Seb later. I feel so wrought up now that he'll only pick up the bad vibrations."

They drove back to the beach quietly through some country lanes, not saying anything, thinking over the experience. Looking idly in the mirror, Tim noticed the truck several times. They were going quite slowly, yet the driver made no attempt to overtake. When he looked for the third time, the truck was still there.

"Anne?"

"Yes, Tim?"

"There's a truck behind us."

"So?"

"He hasn't made any attempt to pass us."

"What are you trying to say?"

"Is he following us?"

"No," said Brian. "It's just idling along. Don't be paranoid."

Anne slowed down. So did the truck.

"It's all rather remote here, isn't it?" said Flower uneasily. She expressed all their thoughts exactly. The lane was narrow and straggling woods grew to the edge of the tarmac. There was a concealed ditch there, narrow but deep. Still the truck kept behind the Renault, speeding up a little now as they did the same.

"When do we get to a main road?" asked Tim.

"Another couple of kilometres."

"If we can just stick it out," said Flower. "I think it's just because we're all nervous and—"

"He's coming alongside." Anne's voice was clipped.

"Passing?" yelped Tim.

"I think so."

But he wasn't. He accelerated until he was parallel with them. There were no bends for a while, but only for a very short while. They stared out – and he stared in. It was the nurse with the gun. But this time his hands were locked on the wheel, and he was grinning.

Suddenly he steered towards them and there was a jarring impact as the truck hit the side of the Renault. Somehow Anne kept a grip on the wheel while she put her foot hard down on the accelerator. He veered in again, there was another impact, and Tim could hear the crunch of torn metal. But still she managed to steer on. There was a bend coming up now, but he showed no sign of dropping back. Suppose someone's coming? thought Tim. They wouldn't stand a chance. Then he saw that the man now only had one hand on the wheel. In the other he held a gun.

"God!" Anne fought the wheel as the truck hit them again.

"What are we going to do?" yelled Brian, for once stung into panic.

Not surprising really, thought Tim numbly. We're

all going to be shot in a minute. For a few seconds the Renault drew clear of the truck as they rounded the bend. The road was clear and Anne pushed the accelerator to the floor. But the truck was following them relentlessly and Tim could see the gun, this time pointed unerringly at Anne through the open window.

Tim sensed that Flower was fumbling for something. What the hell could she be doing? Then he saw that she was holding a small, round, barnacle-encrusted rock. He remembered how Anne sometimes collected interesting stones from the sea-bed when she was diving. It was quartz and the crystal in the centre of it sparkled. Winding down the back window, she lobbed it with unerring accuracy towards the truck driver. The stone struck him a glancing blow on the side of his head. As a result he lost his grip not only on the gun but also on the wheel. But rather than slewing away from the Renault he swerved into it, and with a grinding crunch both vehicles left the road, bounced over the narrow ditch and charged on into the woodland. Their headlong dash was soon halted as they piled into the undergrowth, coming to rest in a jangle of metal and onrush of steam that echoed over the woodland for what seemed like hours. Tim found himself lying on Flower in the back of the Renault while Brian and Anne were trapped in their seats in the front.

"Everyone OK?" asked Anne.

The chorus was in the affirmative.

"But what the hell is *he* doing?" demanded

Flower. Tim, however, was already out of the car and running towards the truck.

"Be careful!" Anne shouted.

The man was half in and half out of the driving seat and his door was open. The gun lay on the grass. There was blood on his face and he seemed concussed, muttering and groaning, his hand searching the seat and the floor for the gun that was no longer there. Tim grabbed it just as the man looked round.

"Give me that!"

"No way."

He lurched out of the truck, taking a staggering swing at Tim. Missing, he was thrown off balance.

"You tried to kill us!" yelled Tim. "Why?"

"Give me that."

"Why?"

"You little—" He swung again and this time fell down. Then his head seemed to clear and he staggered to his feet.

"I'm going to get the police," snapped Tim.

"Yeah?" With surprising agility the man went for him, oblivious of the gun, catching him round the waist. They went down on the grass and Tim felt an intolerable weight on his chest. He was being knelt on.

"Give me that gun!"

"No."

The blood was still welling down the man's face and some of it fell on Tim.

"Give it to me!"

"No," Tim gasped again.

"Want a broken wrist?" He grabbed Tim's wrist and forced it back hard until he could not bear to resist any longer. "Drop it."

The gun thudded back on to the grass and with a painful grin of satisfaction, he scooped it up. With the grin spreading, he put the gun to Tim's head, his finger on the trigger.

"Now you're for it," he said.

There was a metallic click. Tim had already closed his eyes. So this is it, he thought. No more Mum. No seeing Dad come out. No more Green Watch. The click came again. What was he doing? Playing Russian Roulette? Would it hurt? The click came again and again. Then he heard a chuckling sound.

Tim found himself being dragged to his feet and when he opened his eyes he saw a look of grim pleasure on his tormentor's face. "Had you worried," he muttered, rubbing the blood out of his eyes. He pulled him struggling towards the wrecked truck and, holding him by his sweater, began to search in the front pocket. It was only when he had dragged out the little tin box that Tim realised he was searching for more ammunition.

"Stay still."

"No chance." Tim tried to wriggle himself out of his jersey, but seeing what was happening, the man hit him as hard as he could round the head. Tim saw a long black tunnel racing towards him. As he passed out, he could hear the man re-loading the gun.

"Tim?"

"What?"

"Tim!"

"What is it?"

"Are you OK?"

"What's OK?"

"Are you all right?"

"I'm sleepy."

"You had a bang on the head." Anne's voice was insistent. "You must wake up."

Tim gradually surfaced, seeing a blur which slowly sharpened into Anne's face. His head hurt and he felt sick. Then he saw Brian and Flower standing there, looking frightened. "I'm all right," he muttered. Then it all came back to him in an unpleasant rush. "Where is he?"

"Gone," said Brian.

Tim stared hard from one to the other. There was a puffy look to one of Brian's eyes and Flower had a cut lip. Anne seemed to have survived intact until he noticed the bruise coming up on her cheek.

"We had a bit of a scrap," she said by way of explanation.

"But where's he gone?' demanded Tim blearily.

"Into the wood. Legged it," said Brian briefly.

"What about the gun?"

"We grabbed it. He didn't get a chance to load it properly. We jumped him just after he bashed you."

"But—" He was not to finish the sentence as the howl of sirens echoed down the narrow lane.

"How long have I been out?" asked Tim wonderingly.

"About ten minutes – long enough for me to make a phone call," said Anne.

Tim staggered to his feet as the police car and ambulance screeched to a halt.

"This is ridiculous," he muttered.

"What is?" asked Flower.

"I'll be the third member of the team in hospital in as many days." He tried to laugh but winced instead. His head felt as if it was going to split.

"I don't find it very funny," said Anne. "In fact I've never been so frightened in my life."

Tim was kept in hospital that night after he had talked to an almost over-friendly policeman who treated him like a baby. Then, when he'd been checked over by a doctor and pronounced "comfortable", he fell into a deep, dreamless sleep that lasted until he woke the next morning at eight. Anne was beside his bed.

"How do you feel?"

"OK. Bit muzzy."

"They're going to discharge you later when you've seen the doctor."

"Great."

"Tim"

"What is it?"

"The police took down all our statements and they've towed away the vehicles. We'll get ours back this afternoon; they're hanging on to the truck. But apparently it's a maintenance vehicle from the psychiatric hospital, and they don't have anyone on the staff answering to the description of that murderous—"

"They must have. He was a nurse."

"They say not."

"So they haven't found any trace of him?"

"No."

"It's like – like a conspiracy. Us against the rest of the world."

"That's what the others think."

"And what do *you* think?" asked Tim urgently.

"There's a massive cover-up going on," she replied slowly. "I'm sure of it. And it's like a blanket – a suffocating blanket."

Tim nodded. "Are we in – are all our lives in danger?"

"I'm sure of it."

"But the police—"

"They can't help us."

"So we're completely unprotected?" He tried to sit up.

"Lie back. I shouldn't be talking to you like this."

"They're picking us off one by one. Seb, Teddy, me – where's it going to stop?"

"It'll only stop if we can expose what's going on."

"That's why I'm going in."

"*What?*"

"I *want* to do it."

"You're not going into Sea Spit."

"I am."

"No, Tim. I'm not going to let you take that risk."

"And—"

"Someone else is going to do it instead."

"Who?" asked Tim indignantly.

"Someone I know. He's a journalist."

"Look – this is a Green Watch job. We don't want outsiders."

"It's too *big* for Green Watch."

"Cobblers!"

"It *is*, Tim."

"Who is he – this journalist bloke?" asked Tim sullenly.

"Bill Robertson. I knew him when I was diving. He's on the *Guardian*. He'll take it up."

"You mean *he's* going to hide in those dustbin things?"

"Yes."

"He's agreed?"

"I've told him everything. He'll get in there. And they won't dare touch him."

"Why not?"

"He's very well known – almost a household name. He's written a lot of books."

"Good for him," said Tim sarcastically.

"Tim—"

"It's *our* job."

"Listen. I don't want to quarrel with you, Tim. You're meant to be recovering. By rights we should be having police protection."

"They won't give it?"

"None of them believe me. Not really. They accept that we were run off the road—"

"Like Seb."

"They're talking about grudges – maybe from when we were campaigning to save dolphins. But they won't accept the Sea Spit angle."

"So, no protection?"

"Nothing. So I've made a decision."

"Which is—" he asked suspiciously.

"I want you to go home."

"Thanks."

"And the others are going back to Romney Marsh. They're going to stay with Mr Andrews."*

"He's potty!"

"But safe."

"Anne—"

"I'm not changing my mind, Tim."

"Let me go with them. I don't want to go home."

"You're safer split up. Until all this quietens down."

"And you?"

"I'm staying with Seb."

"Where will you sleep?"

"They say I can go on sleeping here."

"And Teddy? What will happen when they discharge him? He's walking straight back into danger."

"I've thought of that and I've persuaded him to go to his brother at Bexhill. Just for a few weeks."

"And you mean he's agreed?"

* *Battle for the Badgers*

81

"He's very shaken up."

"You *have* been busy." Tim's sarcasm was withering.

'Well, I've had to be. I hope you don't—"

But Tim was not to be appeased. "You've sold us out – to this Robertson twit."

"That's what Flower said," she replied ruefully.

"And Brian?"

"He's been pretty quiet."

"Brooding—" said Tim with satisfaction.

"Maybe."

There was a long silence. Then Tim said savagely. "You won't get away with this."

"You make me sound like an enemy."

"What about Seb?"

"You don't think I've asked him, do you? He can't be worried in any way."

"How's he getting on?"

"Well. But we could damage him with all this," she persisted. "Tim, I can see how angry you are."

"Yeah."

"But I can't be responsible for putting your life in danger."

"No, *I* am."

"You're still a child."

"Thanks."

"A resourceful one. But I'm the adult in charge."

"Seb would have let us."

"Would he?" she asked fiercely.

Tim had to be honest. "I don't know – I think so."

She got up. "They'll want to give you breakfast."

82

"I don't want any."

"You must. Tim – you *must* understand."

"Sure. Where are you going now?"

"To ring your mother."

"Why?"

"To get her to collect you."

"No way!"

"You can't take the train back to London. You might still have concussion."

"Then why are they discharging me?" he asked fiercely.

"They wouldn't expect you to take a long train journey on your own."

"Don't ring her."

"But—"

"If you do, I won't go with her," began Tim and then paused. He had suddenly made up his mind and knew what he had to do.

"I insist."

He made a show of giving in. "All right then."

"Thanks, Tim." She stood up. "I'll be back with her arrival time in a minute."

"Hang on—"

"Yes?" She was impatient to go now.

"What are you going to tell her?"

"Very little. That we had a motor accident and that you're fine and—"

"Won't she be angry you didn't call her last night?"

Tim took a malicious delight in upsetting her.

"I should have done. I was just so tired. Anyway, I'm doing it now."

"OK."

"I'll see you in a few minutes."

Tim lay back, determined to carry out his plan. Of course, when he had operated on his own last time* he had got into big trouble. This time he was afraid but determined. Green Watch were in deadly danger, and he was going to get them out of it by exposing Sea Spit. Somehow. Another part of his mind told him he was being incredibly stupid. But he firmly sealed it off.

"She'll be here at lunchtime."

"OK," said Tim grudgingly.

"I'm *very* sorry."

"Can't I see Brian and Flower?"

"Phone them when you get back."

"You mean—"

"They've already gone."

"Blimey!"

"I'm a quick worker." She attempted a feeble joke.

"So I'm to stay here—"

"I'll be with Seb. I'll come and see you when she arrives."

She's got every angle covered, thought Tim. He would have to go home and then come back. He'd invent a call. A new summons. But how would he convince his mother that he had to go back?

* *Dolphin's Revenge*

84

Somehow he would have to, but it was going to be very difficult.

Nothing happened at lunchtime, although Tim was dressed and ready, sitting gloomily by his bed in the side ward he had been put into. At about one-thirty Anne came in, looking worried.

"What's up?" he asked.

"It's your mother. She's gone down with a bout of 'flu. Said it'd been coming on all yesterday and when she went for the train she suddenly felt really terrible. She wants to know if you can stay for another night. She'll send someone down tomorrow."

Tim shuddered. "That'll be Mrs Mings. Mum's friend. She's awful."

"Awful or not, she's coming. It's just that she can't manage today."

This was amazing, thought Tim. Everything was working in his favour. Then he felt ill inside again at the knowledge of what he had to do.

"So – I'm going to stay the night at the *Crown*. And so are you. We'll go across now."

"Yes?"

"We're going to stick together, aren't we, Tim? All the time."

He nodded.

Chapter Seven

Tim lay on the bed at the *Crown* watching television, plotting and planning, as he had done all day. Twice he had tried to ring Mr Andrews' railway yard, but there had been no answer on either occasion. But that meant nothing. Mr Andrews was often out on his land and Flower and Brian were probably with him. Anne sat in the corner, reading a novel.

"How long will Seb be in hospital?" Tim asked.

"Another couple of weeks, and then he's going to have a long convalescence."

"He won't like that."

"He doesn't know."

"But he'll be all right? In the end, I mean?"

"That's what they say."

Tim's eyes returned to the television screen. Then

the telephone rang and Anne answered. She spoke quietly and then put the receiver down slowly.

"Who was it?"

"Teddy. They've discharged him. He's just off to Bexhill."

"So—?"

"He wants to see me first."

"What about?"

"Don't know."

"Be careful," said Tim instinctively.

"It's only Teddy."

"Yes, but—"

"I'll pop over. You stay here."

"I'd like to come."

"I shan't be a minute." She stood up and looked at her watch. "It's five o'clock. We'll have some tea when I get back."

Tim looked up and grinned. He was starving.

"I'm going to lock you in."

"You keeping people out, or me in?"

"Bit of both." She smiled.

Anne didn't come back. Not for five, ten, fifteen minutes. What on earth could Teddy be jabbering on about? When twenty minutes had passed Tim became worried. What was going on? He rattled the door, but as she had said, it was locked from the outside. Trying to stay calm, Tim waited for another five minutes, but still she didn't appear. A wave of panic surged inside him. What was he going to do?

Surely if there had been some problem, Anne would have phoned him? Trying to control the panic he went to the window. It opened easily. He was looking down on to a small yard at the back of the hotel. There was only a short drop from his first floor window and a couple of rickety-looking drainpipes would help him down. Without thinking any more, Tim lowered himself over the sill and within seconds was standing in the yard.

Luckily there was no one to witness Tim's un-orthodox exit and he walked hurriedly through an arch into the foyer of the hotel, which was all panelling and horse brasses. There was no sign of Anne. He raced upstairs, wondering if she had gone back to the bedroom while he was climbing out of the window, but the door was locked as before. Running downstairs, he looked round the foyer again. There were a few businessmen, a tweedy woman with a huge dog and a couple of young men talking about golf in high, excitable voices.

Tim went to the reception desk, the panic rising inside him, practically making him unable to speak.

"Sorry?" said the receptionist as he stuttered something unintelligible.

"Have you seen Mrs Howard?"

"Who?"

"Mrs Howard. She's young with a lot of blonde hair. Very tanned face." He spoke so rapidly that she asked him to repeat the sentence, all the while giving him a very curious look.

"Oh, her."

"Yes?"

"She went out."

"With an old man?"

"Yes, he was with them."

"*Them?* Was there someone else?"

"Young man. Well built. With a moustache."

Tim fell apart. She had just described the nurse. The nurse with the gun.

Tim's head was reeling as he stared at the receptionist.

"Is there something wrong?" she asked, fiddling impatiently with her hair.

"Er—"

"Well?"

Tim just didn't know what to say. He needed advice. "I think she's been kidnapped," he blurted out.

"What?"

"Kidnapped. Taken away."

"Are you having me on?"

"No," said Tim angrily.

"What's going on?" A man in a pinstriped suit appeared behind the counter.

"This young man claims one of our guests was kidnapped."

"Oh?" The manager gazed at Tim with a kind of irritable suspicion.

"Mrs Howard—"

"Mrs Howard? Are you Tim Howard? She gave me a note for you."

"What note?"

"I'm sorry if I've delayed it. I was called away. She only gave it to me ten minutes ago." He produced a hotel envelope and slapped it down on the desk. Tim ripped it open.

Dear Tim,
Sorry to rush away but a man from the CID called. He wants to interview me again re the crash. Taking Teddy with me. Back in a couple of hours. Sit tight. Love, Annette.

"Everything all right?" The man's bland eyes rested on him with the same suspicion.

"It's weird."

"Why?"

"She wouldn't have left me alone."

"No?"

"And why didn't she phone through? She'd locked me in."

"Locked you *in*?"

"And her name's Anne. Not Annette."

"I'm very sorry—"

"I don't like it."

"But why did she lock you in? I really can't understand—"

Tim and the manager stared at each other in total impasse.

"Look," Tim began. But he was interrupted by someone else – a short, rather fat man with glasses and two or three days' growth of beard.

"Excuse me."

"Yes?" Tim and the manager spoke together.

"I couldn't help overhearing. I think I could sort some of this out."

"You could?" The manager beamed.

"The name's Bill Robertson."

"The journalist?" said Tim.

"Yes. I've been in contact with Mrs Howard—"

"Well," said the manager briskly. "Unless other help is wanted, I'll leave you both to it."

"Come over here," said Bill. "I need to know what the hell is going on."

"We haven't got time to talk. She could be in danger. She *is* in danger."

"What do you want me to do?"

Tim shrugged. "She could be anywhere."

"So – tell me fast."

They sat in a small, dim lounge with no one else about, and as quickly as he could, Tim told Bill Robertson of the startling events that had begun to tumble over each other so rapidly. He listened throughout with very careful attention, and showed no sign of not believing him. Eventually, when he had finished, Robertson said quietly, "My God!"

"It's all – pretty unbelievable, isn't it?"

"No."

"You mean—"

"We've had an eye on Sea Spit for some time.

91

There's one hell of a cover-up going on there, and it's authorised in the highest places."

"You mean the government?"

"Top level."

"What are we going to do?"

"Expose them."

"How?"

"Your plan. The one Anne vetoed."

"What about it?"

"You still on?"

"You bet! But what about Anne?"

"They've got her. I'm going to check with the local CID now, but I'm sure they have."

"But they might kill her. I mean – that's what he tried to do to us. Can't the police help?"

"They're not going to believe everything. But yes, they'll look for her."

"And if we tell them she's been taken to Sea Spit?"

"They'll look there too – and get laughed at."

"So—"

"*We're* going in."

"She said I wasn't to—"

"Well, she was trying to protect you. I'm not. Besides, no one's going to do anything to me. I'll leave word at the *Guardian* that I'm going to Sea Spit. That'll create a deadline on me getting out. So *I'm* protecting you."

Tim felt better. But he was still desperately worried about Anne. "They're going to get anyone who knows about the beach. Is Seb safe on his own?

What about Flower and Brian? Where are Anne and Teddy?"

"All this is going to be resolved once we're in – once I've photographed this beach."

Everything depends on evidence, thought Tim. They had had to take photographs on the whaling ship* as well as trying to do the same in the dolphinarium.† He always seemed to be gathering evidence for Green Watch. Dangerously.

"While you're phoning, I'm going to see Seb. The hospital's only just over the road. He'll be expecting her, and he doesn't know what's going on."

"OK," said Bill. It's seven. We'll meet back here at eight. Then we'll drive out towards Sea Spit, leave the car – and see what we can do about those barrels of yours."

"It might mean spending a night in one of them."

"Or I just might find another way in. Can you climb?"

"Yes," said Tim. "I used to be scared of heights, but working with Green Watch – somehow it cured me." He laughed at the thought of something else. "My mum!" he gasped.

"What about her?"

"She's sending her friend down tomorrow to pick me up. Suppose we're still at Sea Spit?"

"We won't be," Bill reassured him.

"But if—"

* *Sad Song of the Whale*
† *Dolphin's Revenge*

"If we *are* still in there, we won't be doing much talking."

"You said no one would touch you, because of the paper and—"

"Only joking," replied Bill casually.

But was he? wondered Tim.

"Seb?"

"Mm."

"How are you?"

He opened his eyes. There were no wires now and he was in a different side ward. There was a pallor to his face and a drowsy, dazed look in his eyes.

"Tired – tired all the time."

"Anne's got 'flu," Tim lied glibly. "So she's not coming in tonight, in case she gives you a germ."

"When's she coming back then?" He looked startled and Tim saw how much he had come to depend on her presence in the hospital.

"Tomorrow."

"In the morning?"

"Oh, yes. If she's better."

Seb searched Tim's face with his eyes. "I've been trying to piece together what's been happening. But there are so many big holes—" His voice died away and his eyes closed.

"Not yet," said Tim. He took Seb's hand and squeezed it.

"Mm?"

"You're not ready yet."

"But is everything all right?" Seb insisted, opening eyes full of alarm again.

"Of course it is."

"Is it over?"

"Is what over?"

"Whatever is happening."

"Oh, yes. All over."

"You sound like a nurse."

"It's the truth," lied Tim. "It's all over."

"Well?"

"I'm ready."

"Know somewhere we can leave the car?"

"Yes. 'Bout half a kilometre away."

"That'll do."

Tim got in Bill's estate wagon. Inside was a pile of rope and climbing gear.

"You a climber?"

"Like you, I've had to learn to be. Had quite a number of dodgy assignments. Like this." He winked at Tim. "Your dad OK?"

"He's not my father."

"Oh, yes. Sorry. You're an adopted Green Watcher, aren't you?"

"Yes."

"I've known Anne for years. Didn't know she'd married Seb."

"They seem very happy."

"Yeah. I've known him vaguely off and on. Bit of a perfectionist, isn't he?"

"You could say that."

"And he cares, doesn't he? Cares too hard."

"So do you, don't you?' asked Tim. "Or you wouldn't be doing this."

Bill laughed. "Oh, I'm after a good story." He paused. "And I don't like cover-ups," he said. "Particularly when they're as powerful as this."

"Do you think the Prime Minister knows?"

"I doubt it. The real power lies with the civil servants – the bureaucrats." He paused again. "They'll stop at nothing."

They drove in silence towards Sea Spit, each preoccupied with his own thoughts.

Eventually they arrived at a lay-by.

"Better stop here and walk."

"Can we get round by the beach?" Bill asked. "I'll feel a bit conspicuous walking down the road with all this gear, even if I put it in a hold-all. It looks a bit purposeful, somehow. Know what I mean?"

Tim did. "We can go over the marshes, then on to the beach."

Bill rootied about in the back of the car and came up with a couple of fishing rods and a tackle box. "How about this for a brainwave?" he said. "I suddenly remembered I've got this stuff."

"We'll have to dig for bait," said Tim.

"What happens if the tide's not out?"

"Then it'll have to be worms," replied Tim.

Dusk had already fallen as they stumbled over the

pebbles near Sea Spit. The bulk of the power station was outlined broodingly against a purple sunset, crouched like some monster feeding by the sea.

"Just a spot of innocent night fishing," muttered Bill as he set down the equipment. They had managed to dig up some unsuitable bait, and while they were atttaching it to the hook, Bill remarked, "The security looks tight."

"There's a spotlight at night," Tim replied. "Sweeps the walls. And security men. They prowl about."

Bill continued baiting the hook while he eyed the stark outline of Sea Spit.

"We'll have to move damn quick."

"Sure."

"We'll wait till the spotlight comes on, but there *is* a place that's possible. See that flat bit of roof with the skylight or whatever it is? It's three – four – storeys up. But there's a gutter. I could get a climbing hook round it. But as I say, we'd have to be pretty damn quick. Then there's no guarantee we can get in. Still want to take the risk, Tim?"

"We've got to. Do you think she's inside?"

"I don't know. Let's hope so."

What he means is that if she's inside she's alive, Tim thought. And if she's not inside – Tim didn't want to think any more about that.

They sat and fished, trying to be patient. Then, when it was pitch dark, the spotlight came on. It began to sweep round the buildings and Bill timed the beam as it hovered over each spot.

97

"It's slower than I thought," he whispered.

"How much time does it give us?"

"About three minutes."

"Can we do it in that time?"

"Sure."

"Really?" Bill had sounded confident but there was still a trace of hesitation in his voice.

"Put it this way – if we don't we're in trouble."

"When?"

"Anytime now."

"What's that mean?"

"Next time round. Leave those rods stuck in the pebbles."

"What about the security men?" hissed Tim. "We haven't seen any of them."

"Should they be patrolling?"

"I don't know; there's usually loads of them around."

"At night?"

"In the day—"

"So maybe we're going to be lucky. Perhaps they think the spotlight's enough of a deterrent."

"But if there's no one to see what's in it?"

"There must be someone sitting at a vantage point. Maybe more than one."

They sat in the wave-rustling silence, fearfully waiting for the spotlight to come round again. Tim noticed one of Bill's hands was shaking. With tension? Or fear? Or both?

Chapter Eight

"Now!"

They were up and running.

"Keep down!"

"OK."

Their slogging footsteps on the pebbles seemed relentlessly loud. Then the terrible scrunching stopped and they were by the wall. How long had they been going? wondered Tim. It seemed like time was ticking away very fast. Too fast. He watched Bill hurl his weighted rope and hook up. Agonisingly it scraped and then fell. He tried again – this time it held. "Get up!" he said.

The rope was knotted and Tim had no problem in climbing up it in a flash. He was followed by Bill, who seemed to take an appallingly long time.

"Come *on*!" Tim hissed.

"Coming."

Tim stole a glance at his watch but he couldn't remember what time they had started. The spotlight seemed horribly close. He almost screamed aloud in frustration.

"Come *on*!"

"Coming," was the steady reply. The spotlight swung even nearer.

They were up – and just in time.

"I may have the equipment," wheezed Bill Robertson, "but I'm definitely losing the energy."

"Now what?"

"That skylight."

Keeping well down, they crawled over to it. There was a glass hatch and, switching on a minute torch, Bill stabbed brief light at it.

"It's a store-room. Boxes and things," said Tim.

"Will it shift?"

He tried. "No."

"And it'll be reinforced. We could be in trouble."

"Do you want to try?" Tim asked desperately.

"All right." He tried. "Nothing – won't budge. Hang on, though. Something's moving." There was a cracking sound and it slid partly open. "Got it!"

"Let's get in fast," said Tim.

They slid down into the store-room and Bill pulled back the shutter. "So much for their security," he whispered.

"Now what?" asked Tim.

"Let's go down, very slowly." He opened the door

gently. "We're in luck. Look." There was a long flight of steps leading down. "I reckon we're in a service area, if we only knew what level to get out on."

"We'll have to take a risk," said Tim. Ever since Bill had made such heavy weather of the climb he had felt less confidence in him. It was unfair, he knew. But that's the way it was.

"The beach has got to be ground level."

"We couldn't walk on to it, could we? Just like that?" asked Tim in rising panic.

"No," said Bill. "We couldn't. And I reckon we're almost at ground level. Let me try this one." He cautiously inched open the door. A long tiled corridor led towards a sign. It read TOP SECURITY AREA.

"Well?"

"Let's go take a look," said Bill. "But we may need protective clothing."

"Steve didn't."

"Don't let's take any risks."

They hurried down the deadened silence of the corridor until it turned a corner. A few metres further on there was a machine, rather like an airport security check except it was flashing a number of different coloured lights.

"You have to put a card in," said Bill. "And then walk through."

"And we haven't got a card." Tim was bitterly disappointed. His confidence had been soaring because of the ease of their entry, and now they would have to go back.

But Bill had something in his hand.

"What's that?" asked Tim.

"A card," he whispered in triumph. "We got hold of one at work."

"How?" asked Tim, astounded.

"Something to do with printers," he said mysteriously. Printers who don't believe in the nuclear industry." He put it in the machine and then handed Tim another. "I'll walk through – you shove yours in."

When they were both safely through, Tim whispered, "How many more of those have you got?"

"Half a dozen." He chuckled. "They give access to all this station's top security areas. Or should do."

The corridor wound on until it ran out at a sliding door with a slot in it.

"Card again?" hissed Tim.

"Yes." Bill had paused.

"What's the matter?"

"There's nothing to say this is a contaminated area." He looked at Tim. "You know what that means?"

He nodded. "You mean we could get a dose of radiation?"

"Yes. But there would be a sign."

"Would there?"

"Absolutely." He put the card in quickly. "Absolutely," he said again as if to reassure himself. The door slid open. He passed through and the door slid back. Then Tim put his card in, and nothing happened.

He put it in again and the door slid open. He ran in,

sweat pouring down his face, only to find Bill in very much the same state.

"I thought we'd been separated." He grasped Tim's shoulder.

"What now?"

The corridor ran on, still well lit but beginning to broaden out at the bottom. They hurried on, both of them uneasy and apprehensive. Eventually they came to a steel shutter set into the wall on the left hand side. There was another card slot.

Let's hope it's the same one," Bill muttered as he put it in. Slowly, noiselessly, the shutter rolled up and he turned to Tim in elation. "How about that?"

They were in a kind of observation room. There were three white walls. The fourth was glass and directly overlooked what at first appeared to be a technicolour jungle.

"It's a picture," whispered Tim.

"Three-dimensional?" retorted Bill. "I'm damned if it is. It's the beach!"

Tim stared at the jungle outside in a stupefied way.

"What beach?"

"The polluted one, thicko!"

"Blimey!"

Jungle was the only description that sprang to mind. Now he was looking carefully he could see pebbles but no water – no tide-line. Instead there was an all-enveloping structure around it which seemed to be made of some kind of alloy. And where the sea should have been there was a kind of dam, made of steel, and it obviously went down below the pebbles for some way. But it was the plant life that really drew Tim's shocked attention. Everything was monstrous – three or four times its original size. Something seemed to have gone wrong with the colour as well, for all the sea plants were a hideously swollen purple, orange, sometimes deep-veined black. Worse still, things were scuttling around at their base – insects blown up too big, a giant rat that crouched and rustled and, worst of all, a couple of huge black crabs.

Tim drew back with an involuntary cry as Bill brought out his camera. He began taking photographs at a frantic high speed.

"Let's get out!" breathed Tim.

"Hang on!"

"Haven't you taken enough?"

"Not yet."

"Those things – they're revolting."

"They're amazing! This is going to finish the nuclear industry for good and all!"

"Come *on*!"

"What's up?"

"I can't stand looking – that's all."

"That could be our world," said Bill, still photographing. "Don't you realise, they could do that to us. Make *us* monstrous."

"That rat—"

"What?"

"That huge rat. It was out."

"It couldn't have been. It's contaminated."

"I tell you, I saw it myself."

"If it could get out—" Bill paused. "We'd be

104

finished. How *could* they get out?"

"They don't get out," said the voice from the wall.

They spun round but there was no one. Just wall. Yet, to Tim, the voice had a vague familiarity. He felt chilled to the bone, reeling with shock.

"What you saw was a coypu. We keep it here for experimental reasons."

"It's you," said Tim.

"Who?" demanded Bill. He was shaking all over.

"It's Watson. Philip Watson. He works here."

"And I've been watching you for – a few minutes. With my colleagues."

"Colleagues?" said Bill.

"It was you, wasn't it?" burst out Tim. "You tried to kill Seb – and Teddy – and us."

"There's a small group of us."

"You mean there's a load of you in on this—" began Bill.

"I said a small group. You've penetrated a top security area, just in case you're not aware of what you're doing. Only a few of us know about the beach."

"How could you work here and *not* know?"

"It's easy. No one comes into this section."

"And the Reapers?" asked Tim.

"They know nothing."

"But you employed them to check the length of the beach, didn't you?"

"We were concerned that – there might be mutant growth."

"Why didn't you check it yourselves?" asked Tim. "What did you tell them?"

"We would be rather obvious. And the Reapers, as you call them, were paid to keep quiet. Paid well. And just told to—"

"Look for anything unusual?"

"That's right."

"So what now?' asked Bill.

"Oh, it'll be easy." Watson's voice was matter of fact.

"Easy?"

"For you to be found in the sea."

"The police are already suspicious," said Bill quietly. "Don't you think you've rather overplayed your hand at accidents?"

"Yes. There'll be a mystery. But it won't be solved. And gradually interest will fade away."

Tim had a nasty feeling he was right. That was just what *would* happen. They were finished. He glanced desperately at Bill, and was surprised to see he appeared calm.

"Tell me, who in God's name allowed this – aberration to come about? And to be maintained?"

"There was a leak. The beach was screened off. Then we watched what would happen. When we saw what was happening, we knew it was worth preserving. To study. To watch."

"But how do these creatures live?"

"They're fed."

"And the crabs?"

"We've put in a simulated rock pool."

106

"You mean you go out there?" Tim was horrified.

"In protective clothing. Yes. Now, if your curiosity is satisfied perhaps you'd like to join our other captives."

Part of the wall slowly slid away. Standing in a kind of plastic bubble were Flower and Brian.

The bubble opened and they walked out into the observation room while the wall slid shut behind them.

"What the hell are you doing here?" yelled Tim. "You're meant to be back home."

"We never went," said Brian. "Remember the barrel idea?"

"Yes—"

"It didn't work," he said quietly.

"Watson!" yelled Tim.

There was no reply.

"Watson!" he repeated.

Still nothing.

The four of them stood silently, looking at the beach.

"No!" said Flower. "It can't be!"

"It's revolting!" Brian turned away.

"You haven't seen it?" asked Tim.

"No." Flower's voice shook. "They kept us in an office."

"How did you get caught?" asked Bill.

"It was me. They took the bins in all right, and we kept quiet and lay low for ages. But then I got more and more claustrophobic – I felt I just had to get some air. So I opened the lid – only a fraction – and a security man saw me." She looked away, bitterly ashamed of herself.

"Did they hurt you?" asked Bill.

Flower shook her head. "No, they treated us like naughty kids. But they wouldn't let us go. Then Watson turned up. He was very angry – said someone had got into the top security section."

"But how did he *know*?" asked Bill. "Those forged cards – they opened the doors—"

"He said there was an alien card being used. The computer told him or something," she finished vaguely. "He took us down to this room and he spoke into a microphone through the wall. We could see what you were doing."

"You mean you could see through the wall?"

"Yes, it lit up."

"Every mod con," muttered Bill. "And now what?"

"You disobeyed Anne," said Tim. "And she's—"

"So did you," Brian interrupted him. Then he said more kindly, "We're going to see Green Watch projects through – we're not kids any longer."

Bill looked at him admiringly. "I think you're amazing," he said.

"Let's hope we go on being amazing," replied Tim. "Right now we seem to be in a bit of a sticky spot." He turned to Bill. "You sure they won't do anything to you? Or us? Or Anne and Teddy?"

"What's that about Anne?" asked Flower.

Ignoring her, Bill looked at his watch. "In a couple of hours the paper'll be sending people down here."

"A lot can happen in a couple of hours," said Flower.

Tim began to tell Flower and Brian about Anne and Teddy.

"So they're somewhere?" she said.

"That's what we think," replied Tim, looking agitated. "And that's what we hope."

"You mean—"

"I mean I'm frightened that they might have done something to them already."

There was a long, tense silence which was eventually interrupted by Bill. "I think they're bluffing. They wouldn't do anything to anyone."

"No?" Brian was unconvinced. "They've got a lot to lose." There seemed no answer to that, particularly when he added, "Look what they've done already."

They thought of Seb and Teddy and Steve and the nurse with the gun. The thoughts were not re-assuring.

Chapter Nine

They seemed to wait for hours, now reduced to gloomy silence. When Tim looked at his watch he saw the time was one o'clock in the morning. How long were they going to be left sweating it out? Then, abruptly, the sliding door began to move. Standing in the entrance, gun in hand, was the nurse. He had a bandage on his forehead and a cut on his cheek.

"We're going for a little ride," he said.

"Listen." Bill Robertson's voice was contemptuous. "You're going to be in big trouble for this—"

The nurse smiled as if quietly appreciating a good joke. Then he said, "You!"

Flower started. "Me?"

"Come here!"

Slowly she walked towards him.

"OK. Anyone try anything and I'll kill her."

"How many of you are in on this?" asked Bill.

"Shut up!"

It was an interesting point, thought Tim. So far there seemed to be remarkably few.

"OK. The girl will stay with me. You lot walk in front. I've opened the security door. You keep going, and do what I say."

They dutifully trooped past him and down the corridor.

"Keep going."

They were heading towards a large double door. The nurse pushed something and it slid open. A minibus stood on the other side. Behind the wheel was Philip Watson.

Watson drove them out of Sea Spit and along the coast road. Then they swung inland for some kilometres while the ground began to rise about them. It was no longer flat and marshy but undulating. They came to some woods and Watson drove the van up a narrow, rutted track that wound uphill until it reached a small crest. He stopped.

The nurse prodded Flower. "Get out."

He followed her closely, the vicious-looking snub-nosed gun in the small of her back. This time they followed him, with Watson bringing up the rear. Tim wondered if he was also armed.

There was a sickle moon high in a swollen night sky and it gave enough light to show they were standing at the top of a steep-sided quarry. A high-banked path led down to a hut. He could just make out the letters above the door: DANGER EXPLOSIVES.

"This is madness!" stammered Bill. For the first time, Tim could feel his fear.

Philip Watson began to speak very slowly. "I didn't want it to come to this, but ever since that damned old fool called you in, it's become inevitable."

"It was Steve – his son – who started all this," stammered Bill.

He seems to be losing his grip, thought Tim.

"Yes," said Watson. "That damned lunatic. Our security was lousy then. I think you'll agree that it's better today."

"Let us go!" Bill's voice broke. "For God's sake, just let us go! We'll protect your damn secret."

"We won't," said Flower quietly. "What you're doing is terrible. And what have you done with Anne – my stepmother – and poor old Teddy?"

Watson ignored her. "You don't seem to understand the importance of what we're doing," he said grandly.

"What *are* you doing?" asked Brian. "How could it possibly be of any value to anyone?"

"Value, you little idiot?" said Watson angrily. "Don't you understand? We've got mutants down there. Dr Grey is studying them."

"Who the hell is Dr Grey?" asked Tim.

"He's a nuclear scientist with a roving commission. A brilliant man."

"Who's paying you a lot of money," sneered Flower.

"We're being paid a bomb," he agreed. "And we deserve every penny, Tom and I."

At last the nurse had a name, thought Tim. Maybe if they kept talking—

He stole another glance at Bill Robertson, but he had completely cracked up and was standing on top of the cliff, shaking and shivering. Tim's heart sank. He was obviously going to be no help at all.

"Get on with it," said Tom. "We've only got a few minutes."

But Watson seemed to want to explain. "Hang on! I don't have to justify my actions – anyone's actions – to this amateur outfit. But I'm sure you'd like to understand how much we prize secrecy – how important it is to protect this project. Dr Grey, myself, Tom – we've actually kept that security area to ourselves. No one knows what's on that beach. No one's going to be allowed to know. And of course he's got top-level backing. Once he's completed his observations, we're going to destroy it. But he needs more time."

"More time to do what?" asked Flower.

"The beach was contaminated years ago. That's why we brought it into the complex. We wanted to see what would happen over a period of time. It's been invaluable."

"What for?"

"To know what would happen if there were more

leaks. To know what would happen if the leaks were controlled."

"What the hell do you mean by that?" asked Brian.

"The cold war may be over," said Watson, "but we still need to know how to use nuclear power. Aggressively. We need to know what we can *do*."

They all stared at him in horror.

"Do?" whispered Bill.

"I mean, if the need arose."

"Who's interested in it?" asked Flower.

"There's a department which needs to know—" His voice tailed away.

"In Whitehall?"

"All we're doing is observe. But it's very important observation. And it can't be interfered with. Not by anyone. That's what we're paid for, Tom and I, to make sure no one interferes. We've got to do our job."

"Why didn't you just kill Steve? Why keep him locked up?" asked Brian.

"Because we thought we could avoid killing. Your appearance ensured we couldn't. So you've condemned him too."

"What?"

"When we've killed you, we'll kill him. It's the only way now."

"What about Anne and Teddy?" said Tim urgently. "You still haven't told us what's happened to them."

"Shut up, Tim! Can't you see they're just trying to torture us?" said Bill. "They'll tell us what they're

114

going to do, but not what they've done already."

"How did you keep that awful beach a secret in a big place like Sea Spit?" said Brian. He was very pale now and Tim guessed that he was trying to prevent himself from thinking about the others by asking a stream of technical questions.

"It wasn't difficult. The chief engineer knows Dr Grey is conducting a longterm experiment and the contaminated beach is out of bounds."

"What about the rest of the beach?" asked Brian. "Isn't that contaminated too?"

"Your Reapers are there to check that," he said quietly.

"All right." Tom's voice had a note of finality in it. "I've got to go in a minute."

"You won't get near Steve now," said Tim. "The police are looking for you. You can't just walk back into that hospital at night and kill him."

"No? You'd be surprised, sonny. The police can only have a vague description and the hospital think I'm taking a few days out of my vacation. Officially I wasn't even there yesterday. I don't think I'm running too high a risk."

"You'd do all this," said Flower in amazement, "just for Dr Grey and his experiments? Just for money?"

"There's more at stake than Dr Grey," said Watson, and for the first time Tim could see fear in his eyes. "If this ever came out, there are some very powerful people in Whitehall who would be facing criminal charges. They're paying us to protect them – at any price."

"Look," Bill's words tumbled over each other. "I'm sure we can come to some arrangement. Absolutely sure of it. I'll say nothing. I could even—"

"Shut up!" said Watson.

"Please, you've *got* to believe me. I'll do anything to—"

"Get them down to the hut." Tom's voice was expressionless. "I've got to go now. I don't know why you bothered to tell them anything, I really don't." He sounded furious as he loped away.

"I told them because I wanted them to know why they're going to die," said Watson. "It's their right."

"Please—" Bill Robertson was weeping openly now. "Please don't do it."

"Pull yourself together!" Flower shouted. "Why don't you pull yourself together? Why don't you even care about Anne? She's your friend, isn't she? Why haven't you been insisting they tell you about her, instead of letting them rabbit on about how much money they've been making?"

Tim looked across at Flower with a flash of admiration. She was so consistently loyal and courageous. For Bill Robertson he felt nothing but a painful mixture of pity and contempt, and when he glanced across at Brian he could see he felt the same. But apart from that, he felt nothing at all – just a numbness that filled his mind and paralysed his body. He felt that if he pinched himself he would

116

sense nothing – that events had got so much out of control that reality had somehow come to an end. There had been other times in his adventures with Green Watch when Tim had felt that he faced the most appalling danger; there had even been times when he had felt he was actually facing death. But now it had really come, Tim could feel absolutely nothing at all.

"Move!"

With Bill Robertson whimpering and the others totally silent, the doomed little party made their way slowly down the track towards the hut.

"You've killed her already, haven't you?" said Brian woodenly. "You've killed Anne – and Teddy."

"You'll see. Now keep quiet."

"You bastard!" Brian stopped and turned round. "You—"

"I have your sister here. Don't do anything stupid."

"Listen," Bill Robertson came in again, "don't give the man any trouble—"

Brian pushed Bill as hard as he could in the chest and he staggered back. "You haven't got any bottle, have you?" yelled Brian.

"I warn you," said Watson in a low, calm voice. "Just keep walking, or I'll do it here and now."

At the door of the hut the whole party stopped.

"Open it," said Watson, pushing Bill forward.

Bill tentatively opened the door and let out a little

whinny of fear. "There's someone else here," he said. "They're – it's horrible!"

"*What?*"

"Why did you do this to them?" Bill jabbered while the others crowded round him.

Flower shouted, "What has he done?"

"*Move!*"

"I can't stay in here – not with this."

"Stay where you are." Watson's voice rose. "I don't know what you're talking about—" He pushed his way forward. Tim screwed up his eyes, unable to see anything in the darkness. He felt a wave of excitement mixed with wild curiosity but no sense of foreboding and wondered why. A sixth sense told him that something had been planned, something was about to happen. But what was it?

He didn't have to wait long to find out. Bill seemed to stagger slightly, lurched and fell heavily into Watson, expertly knocking up his arm. The gun went off at the ceiling. When his head had cleared from the deafening blast Tim could see Watson on the ground. Bill Robertson was punching him in a very accurate, professional way. After a while Watson stopped struggling.

"You timed that well," said Brian. "And you had him fooled all the way."

"You mean – you mean it was planned?" stuttered Tim.

"I was wondering who would suss it out," replied Bill, grinning. "I had to start early and at times I thought I was overdoing it. I mean, wasn't it a corny bit of dialogue?"

"I believed you," said Tim miserably.

"I'm flattered," laughed Bill.

"I'm sorry—"

"You shouldn't be. Thank God it worked for Watson too."

Tim was still very upset. "Brian hit you, Flower yelled at you, but I—"

"I knew they knew. At least I prayed they did. And that they'd act accordingly."

"You had me fooled at the start," said Flower. "I thought you were a right wet prat."

"Me too," added Brian.

"You're just saying that—"

"Stop taking it so hard, Tim," Bill reassured him. "Aren't we lucky to be alive?"

"I didn't feel anything."

"But you're still lucky to be alive. And so are these two—"

"Which two?" Tim stared down into the darkness of the hut. Finally he saw them. Bound and gagged. Teddy and Anne. "Blimey!"

"Yes," said Flower. "Full marks for observation, Tim." But she put her arm round him so that he didn't feel so bad.

"Get them untied," said Bill with the full force of his new authority. "And use the ropes and gags for Watson. Hurry up – he's coming to. I'll look after the gun."

"Wait!" said Tim. "I've just remembered something. Someone."

"Yes," replied Flower. "Steve. We've got to save
him."

"Then we haven't got much time," rapped Bill.
"And we don't have any transport. Get them untied.
Now!"

Pale streaks of dawn gashed the night sky as they half
ran, half stumbled up the track. Teddy and Anne,
stiff, shocked and shattered not only by what had
happened but by the appearance of so many rescuers,
had elected to stay behind and keep an eye on
Watson.

"I'll get the police down to you," Bill had said.

"I thought you two were back at Romney—" Anne
had spoken slowly.

"It's good thing we disobeyed you," said Brian.

"Maybe not a good thing," replied Flower. "But it
was necessary."

"We'll debate that another time," she said grimly.
"You'd better get going."

"Where to?" asked Teddy. He seemed very dazed
and unsure of where he was, or what he was doing.

"We're going to rescue Steve," said Tim. "We'll
bring him back safely to you."

"My Steve? He's in the nut-house."

"Not for long," said Bill.

Now, as they made the final ascent, Tim looked
towards the sea. He could see the distant huddle of

Sea Spit with the searchlight still playing on the walls. In the dawn the low-lying land, the fields, sparse woodland and sea-shore looked innocent. At rest. Even the sea seemed gentle, almost mild. Then he thought of the beach and its horrible jungle of malformed plants and the wretched things that scuttled amongst them. Sea Spit was like an evil monster, crouched and menacing by the shifting sea. It should be destroyed, he thought. At the moment the land around Sea Spit was pure, but maybe they would contaminate that too. And gradually the rest of England. Dr Grey and his observations . . . He didn't see him as a mad scientist from a lousy film. He saw him only as his name implied – a neat little man with a logical mind. Probably with a family. A wife and two kids. A neat little house. Minding his own business. Getting on with his job. Watching monsters on the beach.

"There's a car," whispered Bill, bringing everyone to a halt.

"Where?" demanded Flower.

"It's stationary, and it's been there some time."

"Empty?"

"I'm sure I saw somebody move behind the wheel. Wait – stand still. Maybe I'm wrong."

They stood there, waiting. Then Bill said, "They've moved again. I think they're watching us."

"What are we going to do?" Brian sounded completely exhausted. "Suppose it's Dr Grey?"

The name had an immediate effect on Green Watch and Tim felt cold inside. That neat little man and his monsters. He had summoned up an image in their minds that was quite deadly.

Now they could all see the car. It was a Mercedes, long and sleek and black.

"Keep down now," said Bill. "Let's move on."

But directly they started to walk again, there was a purring sound and the big car began to draw slowly away.

"He's seen us."

"He was watching us, but where's he going?"

"Who said he was Dr Grey?"

"I bet you he is."

There was a whispered outburst from Green Watch. Nothing could be more frustrating than the sudden disappearance of the darkly gleaming car. It fitted all their fantasy ideas of Dr Grey, and now that mysterious villain was driving away into a steely dawn.

"I bet you it wasn't him," said Brian childishly.

Bill looked at his watch. "It's six. We've got to get to the hospital fast. That guy Tom is determined to kill him, and he's not going to make any mistakes this time."

They walked down the gently sloping road for a nerve-racking ten minutes. Then they heard the noise of an engine. It sounded erratic and depressing. Slowly an old truck came into view with a couple of sheep in the back. Bill flagged the ancient vehicle down.

"Yes?" The grizzled face of an equally ancient man stared out.

"Our car's broken down. Can you get us to Grantly? We have to visit somebody at Viewforth."

"The nut-house?"

"The psychiatric hospital."

"At this time of the morning?"

"Elderly relative. She's ill. Bit of an emergency."

The old man nodded, satisfied. "You kids get up with the sheep. You can come in with me, sir."

They clambered in and the rickety old truck lurched into a grindingly slow progress. Tired as he was, Tim could have screamed aloud in frustration. They could be hours.

The sheep kept moving away from them, and Green Watch kept moving away from the sheep. The truck didn't seem to have any springs and bounced crazily over the pot-holed road.

"We'll never get there in time," muttered Tim.

"If he speeds up he'll fall apart," said Flower.

"Do you think that *was* Dr Grey?" asked Brian.

"What?"

"Was that Dr Grey?"

"Can't hear."

"Never mind."

A pale sun was coming up behind Sea Spit, giving the building a toad-like colour. A bird swung in a great arc round the reactor and then suddenly veered away, heading far out to sea.

At last they arrived at the hospital. Scrambling out, thanking the farmer and running through the car park towards the villa took only a couple of minutes. But at the entrance they were stopped by a brisk nurse.

"Can I help you?"

"One of your patients – Steve Cormack – his life is in danger," Flower blurted out.

"Really, young lady? He seems in no danger to me. Steven is in bed and asleep. As he should be at this time."

"Can we see him?" asked Bill.

"Are you a relative?"

"No—"

"Then I'm afraid you can't come in."

"I don't think you heard me," said Flower in a very clear, loud voice. "His life is in danger. Someone is coming here to kill him."

The nurse's mouth opened in hearty laughter, displaying a set of large tombstone teeth. "Oh. I see."

"See *what*?" Bill was in an agony of impatience.

"This is a rag."

"A *what*?"

"The students' rag. It's a bit late in the year, isn't it? Are you collecting for charity?"

"Where is he?"

"I'm afraid I can't possibly let you in, not even for charity. Stop!"

Brian pushed past her and darted down the corridor.

"Come back here, young man," she screeched. "What *do* you think you're doing?"

"This is serious," said Bill quietly.

"It is," she said. "You are trespassing on hospital premises."

"Someone is trying to kill him." He tried to squeeze past her but she completely barred the way. "Iris!" she called over her shoulder. "Iris!"

But Iris did not come and for the next few minutes they all hovered awkwardly on the doorstep with the nurse's indignation rising and Bill becoming more and more abusive. Then Brian came racing back. Behind him came an African nurse.

"There you are, Iris. Where have you been?"

"Looking for Stevie."

"*What?*"

"He's not in his bed. And this young man thinks he knows where he is."

"But the door was locked—"

"And the window's open."

"Please!" yelled Tim. "Let's move. He could be dead."

They searched the woods for half an hour with no success. Finally, with the two nurses still with them, Bill said, "Where else would he have gone?"

"I need an explanation," began the nurse yet again.

"We haven't got time for one," rapped Bill. "He could be in real trouble."

"Where would he go if he was really frightened?" asked Tim.

"I haven't the—"

"Wait a minute," said Iris. "There *is* somewhere. The folly."

"Where's that?"

"It's an old tower – dates back to when this place was a country house. He goes there a lot – says it makes him feel peaceful."

"Where?" asked Bill urgently.

"It's about a hundred metres down there. Follow the road."

Green Watch raced off, leaving the nurses standing staring after them.

"Are they mad?"

"They've come to the right place if they are," retorted Iris, staring at her colleague angrily. "You shouldn't have held them up."

"They could have been anyone," she replied indignantly. "Anyone."

Chapter Ten

The tower was completely hung with ivy. It stood in a small spinney of dusty trees and the silence inside was total. Tim felt like tiptoeing as they walked over dusty barren earth. The stillness made them unbearably tense and, for a moment, Tim thought he could hear the distant sea.

"What shall we do?" hissed Flower.

"Tim and I will go up. You two stay here and we'll shout if we need help."

Now everyone was deferring to Bill, Tim noticed. From being the despised coward, he had become their unquestioned natural leader.

"All set, Tim?" he asked.

"Sure," said Tim. Here we go again, he thought.

But when they got into the base of the tower, they

found the stairs had fallen away into a mass of broken masonry. In their place a rusty iron ladder ran up the side of the wall. Bill tested it with his foot and then put his full weight on it.

"Is it safe?" whispered Tim.

"Yes – so far."

They began to climb until they reached a stone floor through which the top of the ladder protruded.

"Seems OK," said Bill.

They stood in the circular room, feeling a great sense of anticlimax. There was nothing here at all. A glassless window looked out across the marshes towards Sea Spit. The sun was high in the sky now and more intense. The visibility over the marshes was the clearest Tim had ever seen, but there was mist round the power station. Mist? he wondered. There wasn't a trace of it anywhere else. Everything was so bright and clear. But wasn't it too thick for mist? And thickening?

"Bill—"

"Yes?"

"That mist—"

"Over Sea Spit? That's not mist."

"What is it then?"

A siren howled over the marshes and then another and another.

"It's smoke."

"But—"

"The smoke's coming from somewhere in Sea Spit."

"Oh no!"

"And that's the warning siren going up."

"Isn't it – really dangerous? A fire in a nuclear power station?"

"You're damned right it is!" replied Bill. Then he added, "Unless it's controlled—"

"What do you mean?"

"Suppose it *was* Dr Grey watching us?"

"Well?"

"And he knew we were still alive. That his people had failed to stop us."

"He'd think we'd soon be with the police, insisting they went to look at that beach." Suddenly it all clicked into place in Tim's mind. "He's destroying the beach, isn't he? Burning all those plants and creatures?"

"He could be."

"We've got to get down there!" yelled Tim.

"And Steve?"

"What are we going to do, Bill?" said Tim. "We can't leave him."

"Maybe we should. The loss of that beach – the loss of all that evidence – think what could happen if people like Dr Grey were allowed to observe even bigger contaminations."

"That against Steve's life?"

"Maybe it's against hundreds of lives."

They looked down. "Let's get – hang on! Bill, look – it's *him*!"

Bill stared down in horror. Tom was walking out from behind the tower, straight towards Flower and Brian.

They were down the ladder in seconds, running out of the crumbling entrance to the tower. Flower and Brian were staring up at the sky.

"There's smoke coming from somewhere, Tim," Flower said. "Is it from—"

"He's coming!" panted Tim.

"Did you find him?" said Brian.

"Not Steve—" gasped Tim. "Tom! He's coming round the side of the tower!"

They waited, poised for attack. Brian picked up a rock. Bill edged forward. But no one came.

"Where is he?" hissed Flower.

Tim tiptoed up to the corner. No one was there.

"This is ridiculous," said Bill. "We saw him."

"The other side?" enquired Flower, giving way to pent-up laughter. It was so infectious that Tim joined in.

"Shut up, you two!" said Brian, looking round the other side of the tower. "Not a sign," he said over his shoulder.

"This is ridiculous," repeated Bill, beside himself with a sudden, thwarted rage. "Are you sure—"

"Yes," replied Brian. "He's vanished completely."

"We'll check right round the base of the tower." Bill began to go towards the left side of the building. "Follow me and stick together. Don't split up."

They trudged behind him while sirens wailed on the plain below them.

"Wait!" Bill had paused.

"What is it?" asked Flower.

"A grille. I didn't realise this place had cellars." He

tugged at it, but it didn't give and they moved on until they discovered another. He pulled again, and it came away so fast that he fell back on the grass in a heap, and Tim and Flower gave vent to another burst of uncontrolled laughter.

"Will you two shut up?"

"Sorry," they spluttered. Brian tried not to be impatient, knowing that fatigue and tension were making them behave like this, plus the fact that they all knew they should be down at Sea Spit, trying to draw the rescue services' attention to what they were sure lay at the centre of the fire.

"I'm going down," said Bill suddenly.

"Not alone," answered Flower quickly.

"Yes. Alone."

"Don't do what Anne did," she said quietly. "Don't leave us out."

"Look, I can't take the whole damn circus—" He caught their anger. "OK. Make it snappy."

A short ladder led them down to the musty cellar. Flower still had a torch with a run-down battery, but in its feeble light they could see that the cellar was roofed by a series of arches.

"Must have had wine here," said Bill. "It's a real maze." It was, mainly composed of interconnecting passageways.

"Which way?" asked Tim.

"Hang on a bit. Just listen."

They strained every nerve to stand completely still. Then they heard the soft sound of dragging footsteps.

Slowly the dragging came nearer. Tim felt sick.

There was something unhealthy about the sound, as if a wounded animal was crawling painfully towards them.

"What shall we do?" whispered Brian,

"Shush!" Bill was poised to spring out.

It was almost on top of them now. The steps ceased and they could hear light breathing. Then the breathing stopped.

"OK," said Bill. "Put your hands up."

No reply.

"Stand still. I've got a gun."

Still no reply.

"Just don't try anything. I'm coming forward. Use your torch, Flower."

In the dim light of the torch they suddenly made out familiar features. For a moment, Tim couldn't work out whose they were. Then he knew they were Steve's.

He whimpered as he stood there and his face was cut and bruised.

"What's up, Steve? It's us. We're your friends."

"You've got a gun."

"I was only kidding," said Bill gently. "What's happened to you?"

"I should have killed him."

"Who?"

"Tom. He's been around too long." His voice ended on a sob.

"Was he put in to guard you?"

132

"He's been looking after me for a long time."

"As a nurse?"

"He's no nurse."

"Who put him in here?"

"Don't know. Someone up top."

"Civil servants?"

"Probably. Someone in on Sea Spit."

"Did he guard you every day?"

"Not every day. He would look in."

"Did he threaten you?"

"Sort of. But he's here. Somewhere."

"What do you mean?"

"He went outside. I haven't heard him come back."

"Did he bring you here?" asked Flower.

Steve shook his head. "I ran here to hide. But he found me. He took me by surprise and hit me really hard, but then he heard it."

"Heard what?"

"He's got a two-way radio. Something's happened. At Sea Spit. They kept yelling at him, but he wasn't receiving the information well enough down here so he said he'd go back to his car. I should have killed him then but I was too weak, too—"

"Sea Spit's on fire," said Bill. "Or at least part of it is."

"Wait—" Steve raised a finger to his lips. "I thought I heard something."

There was a long, nerve-racking silence. Then Tim heard a click. "It's a gun," he hissed.

"Quick, Flower," said Bill. "Torch!"

133

But Flower's torch had finally ceased to function. No one could see anything.

"Someone's moving!" shrilled Tim.

And there he was amongst them, a knife in his hand, snarling like a crazy dog. With his first slash he brought blood to Bill's shoulder. Tim could see it suddenly in the darkness – a scarlet stain through his shirt that terrified him. But in stabbing Bill, Tom had over-reached badly and as he stumbled, Steve was on him, punching and kicking. Immediately Bill and Flower were on Tom's chest trying to prise away the knife while Brian and Tim pinned down his legs. He swore and cursed and thrashed and kicked, but eventually he lay still, and Bill had the knife in his hand.

"Are you OK?" asked Flower.

Bill felt his shoulder. "It's only surface."

"There's loads of blood."

"Try and stop it while I'm holding him down."

Flower got up and unbuttoned Bill's shirt. Ripping it up she made a thick pad and bandaged it to Bill's shoulder.

"Tie it tightly," he said.

"It's stopped coming through," Flower replied.

"Great. Steve – we'll need something to tie him up with."

"There's some wire back there," said Steve doubtfully.

"Get it." Tom began to swear and curse again until Bill said, "One more word and I'll knock you unconscious. And I mean it." He looked up as Steve disappeared into the darkness to find the wire. "That will make two of them trussed up."

"We must get down to Sea Spit," said Flower. "We must tell them what's in there."

"If it's not been burnt away."

"How can you burn a beach?' asked Tim.

"You can burn what's growing on it, and what's scampering about."

Tim shuddered. Then Steve came back with the wire and trussed Tom up very effectively.

"Gag?" he asked.

"Why not?" said Bill. "He's got a very foul mouth. See if you can find his car keys."

They found the van easily in the car park and piled into it with Steve. In the distance they could see the two nurses, waving frantically, but took no notice and accelerated out of the gates. They hadn't gone very far towards Sea Spit when they came to a road block.

"You can't come any further, sir. There's an incident down the road," said the officious-looking policeman.

"At Sea Spit?"

"I'm afraid I can't say, sir."

"We have vital information," rapped out Bill.

"Oh yes?"

"I'm Bill Robertson of the *Guardian*."

"Yes, I'm sure you are—"

"And I have essential information for the police. I must get through."

"I've been caught that way with journalists before, sir."

"Let me speak to someone."

"I'm afraid we're all very busy, sir. Now, if you'll just back up and turn round—"

"I want to speak to your superior."

"I told you, sir. We're all very busy."

"If you don't, your head'll roll."

"Are you threatening me, sir?"

"He isn't – I am!" yelled Steve as he sprang out of the car.

"You're what?"

Steve dodged, the policeman dived for him, others came running. He evaded the first but was rugby-tackled by another.

"Let him go!" yelled Bill, getting out as well. He was closely followed by Tim and Flower and Brian.

"Stay where you are!" one of the policemen shouted. There were half a dozen of them now.

"You don't understand—" Bill made a desperate last attempt to communicate.

"Stay by the car," said the policeman stolidly. "Stay right where you are."

"George—" said one of the policemen.

"Yes?"

"We have to open the barrier."

"Why?"

"Authorised Personnel coming through."

"Been cleared?"

"On the radio."

"Who is it?"

"A Dr Grey, sir."

The Mercedes purred through the hurriedly shifted road block. Behind the wheel a small neat man waved a small neat hand at the line of policemen. Then he glanced quite casually at Steve – and the rest of Green Watch standing motionless by the van. He smiled and drove on.

"Who the hell's Dr Grey?" asked one of the policemen.

"Oh, I know him," said another. "He's one of the boffins at Sea Spit. I used to see him every day when I was on duty out there. They say he's going to the States."

Tim watched the back of the retreating Mercedes. He's beaten us, he thought.

"Will you give me your attention, officer?" asked Bill. He was quieter now, less agitated, knowing that they would not get through to Sea Spit, or convince anyone, for quite a while yet.

"I'll gladly do that, sir," he returned sarcastically.

"I have to report that Sea Spit contains a highly radioactive contaminated beach with mutations on it, that the mutations are now being burnt, that we have been attacked by Sea Spit security staff, that one of them is now tied up and under guard in a hut in the quarry at the top of the hill, and another is tied up in a folly in— Officer, please take notes," said Bill furiously. "The longer you delay now, the worse it's going to be for you at the enquiry."

"You a nut-case?" asked the policeman.

"No, I'm the nut-case," said Steve.

"Time's running out," said Bill fiercely. "My paper will make a big issue of this delay. At the enquiry."

"The enquiry," grinned George. "What into?"

"Your incompetence," snapped Flower.

"Now look here, young lady—"

"George."

"Yes, Harry?"

"I think we should start taking notes."

"Whatever for?" asked George indignantly. "You off your rocker too?" he added rudely.

"I just reckon we could be making a bit of a mistake."

"You don't really think they're on the level, do you?"

"They might be, George. They just might be."

"At last," said Bill quietly. There was something in his tone that began to alarm even George.

"All right, sir. First things first. Your name and —"

Cutting him short, Bill began to tell him the story.

Chapter Eleven

"It's quite something."

Seb looked pale and wan as he, Anne, Tim, Flower and Brian sat round the Green Watch table in the old converted windmill on the Romney Marsh that was the Howards' home and headquarters. Tim was amazed. Seb had had a letter from the British Prime Minister, asking them all to come to Number 10 Downing Street to have a "chat about their adventures"

"Will we get a medal?" asked Tim.

"Or a knighthood?" asked Anne, grinning at Seb.

"Or a telling off?" said Flower grimly.

"Why should we be told off?" asked Brian. "We got rid of that beach, didn't we?"

"Dr Grey got rid of it," Seb smiled. "But you lot

did pretty well without me. The PM doesn't have anything to thank me for. And then there was Steve—"

"They *are* going to release him from hospital, aren't they?" asked Anne. "So he can live with his dad again."

Seb nodded. "They've agreed," he said.

Everyone breathed a sigh of relief.

"Are we going to be up to this Number 10 business?" Anne looked worried.

"You bet we are," he said firmly. "We won't get asked again in a hurry."

"Please sit down here," said the beautifully suited man, indicating five ornate upright chairs. "You will be seen presently."

They sat down, self-consciously aware that they were not really well dressed – not looking right. At least that was what Tim felt. Green Watch sat in silence, for they all instinctively wanted to avoid a hushed conversation. But they had not been waiting for very long before they could hear soft footsteps. They looked up in anticipation and were surprised to see not the Prime Minister but an elderly man in an expensive suit and an old school tie. Two other men followed him, taking up a position by the mantelpiece while the elderly man sat on a chair in front of them. Bodyguards? wondered Tim.

"So you're Green Watch?" he began, slightly vaguely. Then he warmed up. "Your – exploits are quite remarkable for such a small group."

"Thank you," replied Seb.

Shouldn't he call him "sir" or something? wondered Tim.

"And of course – events rather – culminated at Sea Spit."

"Culminated?"

"Came to a head."

"Yes. They did rather." Seb's voice was quiet. Suddenly Tim felt a twinge of doubt. Just why were they here?

"Your journalist friend—"

"Bill Robertson?" asked Anne.

"Yes." The elderly man nodded. "I – my colleagues – have asked him to use discretion – and not develop his photographs." There was a faint pause. "I'm glad to say he has agreed."

I wonder what pressure they put on Bill? thought Tim.

"I wondered why nothing had appeared in the press," reflected Anne.

"The situation was very delicate—"

"I thought the whole idea was to bring to the public's attention what had happened at Sea Spit," said Seb, and the elderly man raised his eyebrows at the interruption.

"That would be very alarmist." He smiled gently.

"It would be a service to everyone. Surely?" Anne's voice was distinctly cold. "That beach was a monstrosity, and these power stations need constant reliable supervision."

"Exactly."

"Then what's the point of keeping it quiet?" muttered Brian. "The more the public knows, the more careful people will have to be."

"Well, young man, you've certainly got a point," replied the elderly man with forced brightness. "But you see, if public attention were to be drawn to this – unfortunate experiment – considerable alarm would be caused. And this would be unproductive. I'm sure you agree."

"I don't," replied Seb.

"Then we must agree to differ," he said briskly.

"What happens if *we* go to the press?" asked Flower.

"I'm sure you wouldn't be so – thoughtless."

"I think we should," blurted out Tim. "The public should know what happened at Sea Spit and that instead of admitting that something terrible had happened they were "observing" the situation, running risks, experimenting—"

The elderly man gave him a withering smile. "Please let's get one thing clear. If you went, you wouldn't be believed. If you were believed, and there was the possibility of newspaper coverage, we, the government, would stop it at once." He paused, still smiling. "And I have to tell you that if you *did* go to the press – or your journalist friend decided to publish your exploits – then you would be arrested under the Official Secrets Act. Do I make myself clear?"

"Very," replied Seb. "Only thing is, none of us has

ever signed the Official Secrets Act. So surely there is nothing that *can* be done to muzzle us?"

"There is a law," he replied. "And it must be upheld. Whether you've signed or not is irrelevant. We have provision for that."

"I don't understand," said Anne.

The elderly man began to walk towards the door. "Never mind," he said. "We have the situation well in hand." He departed abruptly, leaving one of his colleagues to show them out.

"He's not getting away with that," said Anne. "I'm going back to Bill."

"He *will* get away with it," replied Seb quietly. "And Bill's been silenced."

"You mean you're going to let that civil servant or whatever he is get away with it, Dad?" asked Flower angrily.

"No," he said resolutely. "We shall just go on campaigning on this issue – and all the others. Now we can see what we're up against, we've only just started."

Tim felt partly frustrated, partly overjoyed. They wouldn't be shut up. Not Green Watch. In the end they'd win through. Or at least they'd always make a fight of it. Green Watch would never give up.

GREEN WATCH

GREEN WATCH is a new series of fast moving environmental thrillers, in which a group of young people battle against the odds to save the natural world from ruthless exploitation. All titles are printed on recycled paper.

BATTLE FOR THE BADGERS by Anthony Masters
Tim's world has been turned upside down. His dad's in prison, his mum's had a breakdown, and he's been sent to stay with his weird Uncle Seb. Seb and his two Kids, Flower and Brian, run Green Watch – a pressure group that supports green issues. At first Tim thinks they're a bunch of cranks – but soon he finds himself entangled in a fervent battle to save badgers from needless extermination . . .

SAD SONG OF THE WHALE by Anthony Masters
Tim leaps at the chance to join Green Watch on an anti-whaling expedition in the Falklands. However, events don't turn out quite as he expected. And soon, he and the other members of Green Watch, find themselves shipwrecked and fighting for their lives . . .

MYSTERY THRILLER

Introducing, a new series of hard hitting, action packed thrillers for young adults.

THE SONG OF THE DEAD by Anthony Masters
For the first time in years 'the song of the dead' is heard around the mud flats of Whitstable. But this time is it really the ghostly cries of dead sailors? Or is it something far more sinister? Barney Hampton is sure that something strange is going on – and he's determined to get to the bottom of the mystery . . .

THE FERRYMAN'S SON by Ian Strachan
Rob is convinced that Drewe and Miles are up to no good. Why else would two sleek city whizz-kids want to spend the summer yachting around a sleepy Devonshire village? Where do they go on their frequent night cruises? And why does the lovely Kimberley go with them? Then Kimberley disappears, and Rob finds himself embroiled in a web of deadly intrigue . . .

Further titles to look out for in the Mystery Thriller series:

Treasure of Grey Manor by Terry Deary
The Foggiest by Dave Belbin
Blue Murder by Jay Kelso
Dead Man's Secret by Linda Allen
Fighting Back by Peter Beere

HIPPO BESTSELLERS

PRESS GANG

Why not pick up one of the PRESS GANG books, and follow the adventures of the teenagers who work on the *Junior Gazette*? Based on the original TV series produced for Central Television.

Book 1: First Edition
As editor of the brand new *Junior Gazette*, and with five days to get the first edition on the street, the last thing Lynda needs is more problems. Then an American called Spike strolls into her newsroom and announces he's been made a member of the *Gazette* team too . . .

Book 2: Public Exposure
Lynda is delighted when the *Junior Gazette* wins a computer in a writing competition. But she can't help feeling that it was all a little too easy . . . Then articles for the *Gazette* start to appear mysteriously on the computer screen. Who is the mystery writer, and why won't he reveal his identity?

Book 3: Checkmate
It's midnight, and Lynda's got to put together a whole new edition of the *Junior Gazette* by morning. The only way she can do it is to lock the office, keeping her staff in and their parents out! Spike's supposed to be taking a glamorous new date to a party – how is he going to react to being locked in the newsroom for the night?

Book 4: The Date
It's going to be a big evening for Lynda – a cocktail party where she'll be introduced to lots of big names in the newspaper business. There's only one problem: who's going to be her date? The answer's obvious to most of the *Junior Gazette* team, but Lynda is determined that the last person she'll take to the party is Spike Thomson!

THE STEPSISTERS

When Paige's Dad marries Virginia Guthrie from Atlanta, she's thrilled that he's found someone to make him happy. But how will she get on with her new stepbrother and stepsisters? Especially Katie, the beautiful blonde fifteen-year-old, who looks like a model and can charm her way out of anything!

1   The War Between the Sisters   £1.75

Not only does Paige have to share her room with her stepsister, Katie, but then she finds that Jake, the boy she's fallen in love with, finds Katie totally irresistible. Paige's jealousy leads her to do some pretty stupid things to get her own back . . .

2   The Sister Trap   £1.75

Paige is delighted when she gets a job working on the school magazine. Especially when she becomes friendly with the magazine editor, Ben. But her jealousies over her beautiful stepsister, Katie, flare up again when Ben starts taking a lot of interest in Katie's swimming career.

3   Bad Sisters   £1.75

There's a rumour going round that Mike Lynch, the swimming champion, is cheating at school to stay on the team. And when Paige investigates the story for the school newspaper, she suspects that her stepsister, Katie, might be helping him. Should she find out the truth, even if it means getting Katie into trouble?

4   Sisters in Charge   £1.75

Paige is horrified when her dad and new stepmother announce they're going away together for a week. It means that she and Katie, her glamorous, popular stepsister, will be on their own together for the first time. Taking their past difficulties into account, Paige knows it won't be easy. But things turn out even more traumatic than either stepsister had suspected!